The Lincoln Promise

JAMES BROWN

ISBN 978-1-0688213-0-1
First edition 2024

Cover design by Fresh Design.
Cover photo courtesy of Brian Erickson, Unsplash.

The Lincoln Promise

JAMES BROWN

Published by James Brown

1

Yesterday (Day One)

In retrospect, as I think back just one day, I should have just said 'no' to the courier driver, or taken out a felt pen and written 'return to sender' on the box, and sent it right back to where it came from. But sometimes ignorance, coupled with curiosity, and perhaps a small dose of goody goody for me, gets the better of us all.

I mean who doesn't feel excited when they get a free gift in the mail? What is it they say about getting a personal e-mail... a hit of dopamine? I guess that is what this surprise courier delivery did for me.

Anyway, I accepted the package, just a small cardboard box about fourteen inches by twenty inches by six inches deep, hurriedly made a cup of coffee, and sat down in my den to open the box.

I was in my den packing for an impending trip to England, while simultaneously watching one of the States' top current events programs, 'America Tonight,' when the courier driver rang the doorbell. I was more than just a little bit engrossed in the show. The subject was a review of the expected top contenders for the U.S. Presidential election, the traditional first Tuesday in November, some thirteen months hence.

Even though I am a Canadian, I follow the U.S. political, social and cultural environment closely. As a reasonably well informed individual I believe it important to see what our friends down South are up to.

In watching the interviews with the two Senators most consider the top contenders for the next Presidential election I was struck by the level of polarization in the world today. Of the two contenders, one is Senator Jefferson Murchison from California. The other is Senator Layton Conrad from South Carolina. It seems to me that Murchison is Left of Left while Conrad is Right of Right. What is going on in the world these days?

I know that the earth's movement is influenced by centrifugal force. This is a scientific fact. Anyone who plays golf and lips out a twelve inch putt and sees it rim the cup and then fly out two and one half feet away knows this effect. But these days it seems centrifugal force is driving politics as well. The more an issue engages strong interest, the more it seems to move people away from centre. The people with the loudest, or most media centric, voices seem to want to move as far left or right as they can and are taking millions of people with them on their journey from middle ground.

Whatever happened to compromise? What about finding what is best for everyone, not just what is best for your political base? Is anyone paying attention to how far apart people's ideologies seem to be from each other these days? Being negative seems to be the new positive. Where does it all end?

Well, in my case it ended, at least for the time being, with the courier and the doorbell.

From what I saw when looking around, my den was a bit of a disaster area, strewn with clothes, golf gear and miscellany as I am due to leave for the U.K. in just a few days. I have arranged a few nights in London for some sightseeing, good food, and a night at the theatre and then off to Alnmouth, in Northumberland, for a week of walking some of the world's best (and dare I say uncluttered with people and litter) beaches and hopefully four or five rounds of links golf.

I go to the U.K. often. While I love London, I also love wandering the moors and dales of the northernmost counties. I have been to the U.K. at least twice a year since I lost my wife a little over three years ago. On my own now, and the lucky recipient of early retirement, I am free to roam and wander as I like, as long as I make arrangements for my 11 year old Jack Russell Terrier, appropriately named Jack or sometimes, when I am cross at him, just JR.

Our children, no longer kids, are 33 and 29 respectively and don't need me so much anymore. Both of them are happily married, each blessing me with a grandchild. The eldest, our daughter, Susan, and her husband, Tom, have a boy, Jordan, who is 11. Our son, Aaron, and his wife, Becky, have a daughter, Jenny, who is 8.

If you are curious enough to do the math on Susan being 33 and my being 53, it all comes down to honeymoon pictures and baby pictures on the same roll of film.

My wife Em (Emily) and I met, as the Brits would say, at Uni. I was studying Political Science with a minor in History. Em was enrolled in Education and, after graduating, made a career out of teaching Primary School, grades one to three. We were married while still at Uni. It was a small and rather physiologically hurried wedding ceremony. The bride hurrying down the aisle before her water broke.

Em, Susan, and I, lived in student res for a couple of years until graduation. Em and I were then able to find permanent work which allowed us to find a place off campus.

Em loved teaching and was brilliant at it. She was still teaching when COVID struck. You would not believe the lovely notes and hand drawn pictures we got from her class once she became so ill. So heartwarming! I kept every one! Her students loved her.

We always invested wisely, both of us getting into the stock market while still at Uni. We made a few good real estate deals when changing houses over the years. I got a healthy settlement when I opted for redundancy from my Senior Public Service job and got immediate access to a generous pension. Of course we had

Em's income and I get a small survivors' pension from her former employer. A part time gig teaching three or four courses a year at the local university keeps me in pocket change and keeps my brain in good order by dealing with millennials and Gen Zs in class.

As for why Alnmouth, almost twenty years ago Em and I were taking a train from London to Edinburgh and, looking out the window just a few minutes north of Newcastle, we saw the most beautiful sea side village as we slowed through a train station. This village was Alnmouth and we both vowed to visit someday. Em and I were able to do so about ten years ago. We made some very good friends there and I still see them on every visit. I have been each year since except when COVID halted my travel plans in more ways than one.

You see, Em was hit very hard with the first waves of COVID and, already having severe immune deficiencies, I lost her, we lost her, the kids and me, very early in 2020. The pandemic was so new to North America I don't think the doctors or the hospital had any clue how to respond. We were married for over thirty years, all of them wonderful. Her passing hit me very hard as one would expect. This was what prompted me to so quickly opt for redundancy when the opportunity arose. I was at a crisis point in my life and walking away seemed the best way to cope.

We were married in June of 1990 a few mere months before Susan was born. As my Dad said at the time, "Susan was born with a broken arm trying to hold off until after the wedding."

But enough of sad times and past events! Back to my talking about my upcoming trip, Alnmouth, and my love of the North East of the U.K, oh, and most importantly my surprise package. I have to stop digressing. I best get on with my tale. Get on with my 'tale!' Who do I think I am? Geoffrey Chaucer?

First, Alnmouth and golf. The golf around Alnmouth is wonderful. There are these true links courses where you get to play with locals who love the game. As an added bonus, or bonuses, you then get the best advice from locals for the best way to play the courses; the best local fare to dine on, be it fish and chips, a plowman's lunch, steak and kidney pies etc.; and the best local pubs to try the exceptional local ales.

While I have nothing against the great English, Irish, Welsh and Scottish links courses, I have played many; you are just as likely to get paired up with someone from Delaware, Denmark or Brazil whose principal interest in many instances is not golf but to scratch things off their bucket lists. The golf and the local colour are not often the primary goal for many players on these famous courses. Don't get me wrong, play every famous course you can, but gravitate to the lesser known local courses as well. You will not be disappointed.

Even though I am an avid Anglophile, I profess to not liking to drive on 'the wrong side of the road.' In Alnmouth I can actually reach five eighteen hole, hidden gem, links golf courses by local bus, most in under 15 minutes, bemusing the locals as I climb off and on the bus, toting my bag of clubs. Always a great conversation starter!

To make matters even better, the bus costs just a few quid. Plus I can walk about two minutes from the cottage I usually rent in Alnmouth and play a nine-hole golf course that is the oldest of its type in England. This little course was established in 1869. What is not to like?

Comfortable in my lazy-boy chair, with my coffee beside me and surrounded by the packing mess, it was time to get back to the mystery box...

After cutting through what seemed like about two inches of duct tape and scotch tape I finally got a look inside this mystery box. Why do people feel the need to ensure all but the most skilled breaking and entering thief can open their packages? I think people purposely pack so you can't open their parcels. Perhaps it gives them some sense of smug self-satisfaction. I can just about hear, "Ha, I sure made that bastard work for what I buried inside the box!"

Once I opened the box there was not really all that much to see but a pile of old papers and a few dozen early twentieth century photographs. But my curiosity had now been piqued as, on top of this pile, is a letter addressed to me. The letter is from the executer of a will. It seems that through the will of a distant relative of mine (of ours, as I have a brother and 3 sisters), I have been left the contents of the box as a secondary bequest.

To explain about distant relatives, my oldest sister, Maureen, since sadly passed away, had a keen interest in genealogy. There were five of us kids in the family. I have a brother and have/had three sisters. Sadly, we lost Maureen to cancer over ten years back. The other three siblings are, thankfully, very much alive, as I am most days.

To digress (again), there are many benefits in coming from a large family. Having three older sisters was a real boon to my development. When in my teens there were always lots of pretty girls around when their friends visited. So I got to have lots of teenage crushes on 'older women'. Older sisters like to dress you in the latest fashions so, when I got into my later teen years, they always made sure I looked sharp. They were working by then and buying clothes for themselves as well as for me. Older sisters make sure you listen to the latest popular music and they take the time to make sure you learn how to dance without looking like too much of a dork. Perhaps most importantly, they know how to keep you in your place so you learn to be nimble and quick witted. Being quick with a retort was the only way to survive their frequent teasing. I think I am quick witted today as a result. The negative, without a doubt, was hand-me-down clothes. Coming from a lower middle class clan I always tell people I was thirteen before I got a pair of pants with the zipper in the front.

Sorry for the digression. I do this too often, as I have previously stated. Back to my sister, Maureen, and how I ended up with this box. As I said, Maureen had a keen interest in genealogy, not just any genealogy but that of our family, the Alexanders of New Brunswick, Canada. Genealogy is a passion I also share with Maureen.

Maureen was always focussed on whatever task she took on. She was a true force of nature. Not content with using the myriad of web-sites and/or paid researchers available she took a much more personal approach in her genealogical search. Often, when she found a connection, she would write to the other party to gather information but, more importantly, to also establish personal relationships. One letter often turned into several epistles back and forth. I think these personal relationships were even more important to her than was the family history uncovered.

She connected with distant, or not so distant, cousins; with hither-to unknown aunts and uncles, etc. Sometimes these relationships developed into friendships and even home visits at her home in Vancouver, in their homes in the Canadian Maritimes or, at times, even in the States or abroad in the U.K. She spared no detail nor lost any opportunity to be as thorough and as unifying as she could be in bringing disparate and unfamiliar family members together.

One such relationship she established was with a... I don't know... sixth cousin twice removed or some such designation. I never really understood how all this works. I am a big picture guy, bored or overwhelmed with too much fine detail. Anyway, let's call them our sixth cousin twice removed. This person left something for Maureen in their will. It seems my name had somehow also become known to this distant cousin's family so this mysterious package was sent on to me as the newly designated beneficiary.

I need to digress here for a third time (or is it a fourth—who's counting) but this departure is important.

One of the fallacies associated with genealogy is that you follow a straight line back as far as you can go keeping with your father's or mother's surnames, usually the father's. In reality following a straight line back could not be further from the truth.

You see everyone has two parents (by blood anyway) and hence four grandparents. Each of these relatives, in turn, has or had two parents and four grandparents etc. After only a few generations you have got thirty-two different lineages to trace. I recently read that for each ten generations that you go back the number of ancestors will be multiplied by a thousand. If you were to go back twenty generations (about four hundred to five hundred years) you'd have over a million great, great, etc. grandparents.

I would say genealogy is as much an exercise in breadth or width as it is one of depth. The research my sister did, and the work I followed up on using more current computer generated techniques, led us to find we were not just Scottish but of French (Norman, Breton and Parisian), English, Welsh, Irish and even some Spanish descent.

We traced one line back to the court of Charlemagne. We have a distant connection to Eleanor of Aquitaine. We found connections to knights from the Norman Conquest with some evidence, albeit vague, that the Harry Potter Castle in Alnwick and several other castles up near Alnmouth were in our family some eight or nine centuries ago. Oh, and Robbie Burns is a sixth great uncle through marriage. I even enjoy haggis and the bagpipes.

I am getting to the mystery box. Be patient!

Our North American connections were mostly seventeenth and eighteenth century immigrants to the then New World, settling in New York, New Jersey and Massachusetts. One of the families had a very prominent leadership role in the Massachusetts Bay Colony. Another relative was a judge in the Salem Witch Trials. As you can see, the further you go back in the family tree the more interesting some of the 'branches' are.

I don't know if it is good or bad for us Alexanders but it seems that most of the various lines of New Englanders in our family chose to fight for the English during the American Revolutionary War. Hence they were stripped of their lands and forced and/or chose to accompany the 'fleets of 1783' up to New Brunswick leaving behind, in some cases, large and well developed farms and, in other cases, important positions in politics and the military.

Some other ancestors stayed and either fought on the side of the Continental Army or integrated into the post war Colonial society. Those that stayed naturally became part of the fabric of the new United States of America. It is through one line of our ancestors that chose to remain stateside which eventually led to the contents of the card board box I inherited.

After reading the cover letter in the box and weeding through pictures of great uncles and great aunts I had no prior knowledge of, I came across a several pages long, well detailed, family tree diagram. You know the ones I mean. We have all seen dozens of these types of diagrams, each showing son of, daughter of, spouse of etc., and dates of birth, death and marriage.

It so happens that one of our family lines that chose to stay in the new United States of America, after the end of the Revolutionary War in 1783, leads to a direct blood connection with Abraham Lincoln. Yes, that Abraham Lincoln, the gentleman well known by all but a few of the poorest informed in this big wide world.

My so called 'sixth cousin twice removed' laid out, on paper, a very clear blood line from one of my early New World relatives to 'Honest Abe'. While this is quite a surprise it really shouldn't be. I read somewhere the other day, in a sometimes questionable web-site, that every US President, save Martin Van Buren, can trace their lineage back to King John of England. Given what I said earlier about the breadth and width of family lines this is not beyond belief. I wonder how many of these Ex-Presidents, besides Abe, would be lucky enough to be related to me?

Kidding aside, the designation 'Honest Abe' requires one to again reflect on the state of politics in the world today, especially focusing on the word honest. First there was George Washington's, "I cannot tell a lie". Thomas Jefferson is quoted as having said, "Honesty is the first chapter of the book of wisdom." And then

Harry S. Truman saying, "The buck stops here." Revisiting these past great leaders should now oblige us to return to more current politicians around the world and ask where did the honesty go?

I understand, by having spent many years in a leadership role myself, that one must make some very difficult choices but giving up honesty or integrity should not be amongst of them.

I know quite a bit about my recently revealed relative, Abraham Lincoln. I studied American History as a Minor at University and among my courses was one on the American Civil War. I recall this as one of my favourite courses and made even more interesting and memorable by the fact our professor was from Mississippi. I must have read a dozen books on the war and about Lincoln during that semester alone. I did quite a bit of research on this era and wrote several papers. If I recall I got an excellent mark in this course.

Lincoln was known for a great many things and amongst the more notable are the Emancipation Proclamation leading to the freeing of slaves, his successful guiding of the Union Army war effort during the Civil War, his saving or preserving the Union, and, of course, 'the Gettysburg Address.'

Like his predecessors and those that followed, Lincoln also issued numerous Executive Orders. According to Presidential records, Lincoln issued forty-eight Executive Orders in total during his time in office. However, if what I found in the bottom of my recently acquired cardboard box is real, and not a forgery or hoax, he issued forty-nine Executive Orders, not forty-eight.

So what was in the box and how did it lead to my current predicament. To understand this let me explain by revisiting some of my University learnings about Lincoln. Is there no end to my digressing?

Perhaps Lincoln's most impactful written words were in the Emancipation Proclamation. The main points of the Emancipation Proclamation can be understood by reading its second paragraph as follows. This is a direct quote:

> *"That on the first day of January, in the year of our Lord one thousand eight hundred and sixty-three, all persons held as slaves within any State or designated part of a State, the people whereof shall then be in rebellion against the United States, shall be then, thenceforward, and forever free; and the Executive Government of the United States, including the military and naval authority thereof, will recognize and maintain the freedom of such persons, and will do no act or acts to repress such persons, or any of them, in any efforts they may make for their actual freedom."*

The intent of this proclamation is clear but Lincoln also had to understand that, in truth, the over-arching goal of the Union Army and of his Presidency was to maintain the Union. Take into account that part of this challenge, as is a challenge in any revolution or civil war, is to consider what happens to the defeated or conquered after victory. In other words how does one reintegrate the defeated back into the so-called 'fold' and let them know they are welcome back. The defeated, in a civil war, are citizens too and they are part of the future. In all but the most genocidal conflicts this has to be a major consideration of the victors.

To digress again for a moment, and to illustrate the importance of post-victory reconciliation, it makes one wonder how Russia can so aggressively covet Ukraine that it is prepared to destroy Ukraine's economy, infrastructure, culture etc. in order to welcome it back as part of Russia. If Russia were to win what have they left that is undamaged or unbroken and what would they need to do to rebuild the country and to embrace the defeated Ukrainians?

Lincoln therefore had competing pressures to deal with but, paramount to him, was 'the preservation of the Union.' To try and further illustrate, reputed to be one of Lincoln's constant detractors was Horace Greeley, editor of the New York Tribune. It is said that Greeley believed Lincoln was lethargic in his policies toward both slavery and the war, and used his newspaper as a vehicle to promote his belief that the President was ineffective. This reputedly helped spur Lincoln on to action. In response, at least in part to Greeley, Lincoln wrote the following in a letter dated August 22, 1862:

> *"As to the policy I 'seem to be pursuing' as you say, I have not meant to leave any one in doubt. I would save the Union. I would save it the shortest way under the Constitution. The sooner the national authority can be restored; the nearer the Union will be 'the Union as it was.' If there be those who would not save the Union, unless they could at the same time save slavery, I do not agree with them. If there be those who would not save the Union unless they could at the same time destroy slavery, I do not agree with them. My paramount object in this struggle is to save the Union, and is not either to save or to destroy slavery. If I could save the Union without freeing any slave I would do it, and if I could save it by freeing all the slaves I would do it; and if I could save it by freeing some and leaving others alone I would also do that."*

Note this was written just one month before the 'Emancipation Proclamation' was issued by Lincoln. It is evidence of his desire to keep the United States of America whole and to save the Union and to respect and recognize the needs of all U.S. citizens, not just northerners. But also in his Emancipation Declaration he had laid out his need to consider the rights and needs of those enslaved or formerly enslaved. Save the Union, free the slaves and reembrace or welcome back the defeated southerners as well. Quite a balancing act for anyone to undertake

To further demonstrate his desire to keep everyone happy, on April 16, 1862 President Abraham Lincoln signed the 'Act for the Release of certain Persons held to Service or Labor within the District of Columbia' into law. This act gave former slave owners in D.C. $300 per enslaved person they set free. More than thirty-one hundred enslaved persons had their freedom paid for in this way, for a total cost in excess of $930,000, almost $25 million in today's money.

In contrast, the formerly enslaved received nothing if they decided to stay in the United States. The act did however provide for an emigration incentive of $100, around $2,683 in today's dollars, if the former enslaved person agreed to permanently leave the United States...presumably bound for Liberia in West Africa.

Finally, yes finally, I return back to the box and its contents.

After learning of the familial connection with Lincoln I read, in detail, the very last document at the bottom of the box. What I found, I am sure, would not have surprised Pandora herself. The last paper I found in the box was an Executive Order, apparently his 49th such Order, and signed by Lincoln on the very day he was assassinated, and reads in part:

> *"I, Abraham Lincoln, President of the United States of America, do hereby proclaim and declare on this day, April 14, 1865, that effective on the first day of May in the year of our Lord, one thousand eight hundred and sixty-five, all persons currently held as slaves within any state of the United States of American, or held as a slave at any time since the outbreak of this recent Civil War, shall be entitled to due recompense. In accordance with the words and principles outlined in the Constitution of the United States of American which reads in part, 'all men are created equal.' I hereby decree that all those who have been held as slaves in these United States, as described above, shall, of necessity and of fairness, be compensated for the harm done to their person, as follows:.*
>
> *Citizens in those States that elected to secede from the Union who, at the outset of the War, held slaves shall be held accountable for the irreparable harm done to those they enslaved. Landowners who employed slaves as part of their agricultural or commercial endeavors, and who owned acreage in excess of 500 acres shall be entitled to retain only 100 of those acres. The 100 acres to be retained shall be determined by that land owner. The remaining land shall be divided by granting 10 acres of freehold to each enslaved male aged 18 and older. These acres are free and clear and are henceforth the property of the former enslaved person now and in perpetuity in accordance with the laws of these United States. If the total acreage available does not allow 10 acres per male recipient, they shall be given an equal share of what is available. Once this acreage has been transferred to the new owners, any remaining lands will be retained by the original owner as additional lands to their allocation of 100 acres.*

Any citizens of these United States that held slaves but owned less than 500 acres of land shall retain one-fifth of those acres. The one-fifth to be retained shall be determined by the land owner. The remaining land shall be divided by granting 10 acres of freehold to each enslaved male aged 18 and older. These acres are free and clear and are henceforth the property of the former enslaved person now and in perpetuity in accordance with the laws of these United States. If the total acreage available does not allow 10 acres per male recipient, they shall be given an equal share of what is available. Once this acreage has been transferred to the new owners, any remaining lands will be retained by the original owner as additional lands to their allocation of the original one-fifth.

Of each former enslaved person due compensation, as cited above, they and their family shall also receive $200 dollars. Said due amount is to be paid at once and by the landholder and shall not, under any circumstance, be forfeit. If not paid at once the amount owing will remain until paid in full at a rate of 5% penalty per annum, until the full amount is paid.

Lastly, any enslaved males over the age of 18 who have not been compensated above but were enslaved to work solely as domestics or similar endeavors are entitled to compensation at the amount of $350. Said due amount is to be paid at once and by the slave holder and shall not, under any circumstance, be forfeit. If not paid at once the amount owing will remain until paid in full at a rate of 5% penalty per annum, until the full amount is paid."

I knew right away that if this Executive Order is a valid document it would hit the U.S. like a thunder bolt. If I recall my university days there were several million slaves in the US in 1860. A quick internet search showed that according to the 1860 census there were 3,952,838 slaves in the USA at that time. Interestingly there were more than one-hundred thousand slaves in the North. In some of the Southern States the slave population exceeded the white population.

My head was spinning with the myriad of ramifications that this document carries. Political, economic, cultural and social issues abound. I needed to take some time to digest all this and then think about what to do. I quickly formulated a bit of a plan for what's next. As I struggled to gather myself I realize the evening had gone. As it was now late, I tried to turn my mind to other more mundane things but never really forgetting what I had just uncovered nor not really ceasing to contemplate what I had to do next.

Despite a glass or two of a sixteen year old Lagavulin, my favorite single malt whisky, I did not sleep well. Rolling around in my head were the various realities of what this document said, whether or not it could be authentic. If yes, what might this mean in an often divisive and polarized political climate and, most pressing, what do I do about it?

2

Day Two

I wake up early which is unusual for me as, since my teenage years, I have always been loath to get up too soon. I don't actually sleep in, but I do like to lie in bed and contemplate the state of the world, the state of my life and, it seems more frequently of late, the state of my love life, or, more to the truth, lack thereof.

Based on yesterday's surprise package, I have even more to contemplate than usual while lazing in my bed. Lincoln, and his promise to the people, dominates my thoughts. So no time for thinking about my love life, or much else, other than this dilemma I face. While I desperately want to enjoy my upcoming trip abroad, I have a document of potentially enormous consequences to deal with.

A sharp bark from Jack downstairs reminds me that I have duties to fulfil. After feeding Jack and letting him outside in the yard to do his business and, to quote Nuke LaLoosh from the movie Bull Durham, "Announce his presence with authority," I turn my attention back to me.

I head to the washroom to begin my daily ablutions, pausing to admire myself in the mirror and not being totally displeased to see who is looking back at me.

As a 53-year-old, now sadly single man, I think I look pretty good. Thinning but still present hair, still blonde, or is it sandy gone gray? My recently renewed passport now describes it as sandy not blonde. Is that a sign of things to come?

Bright blue eyes look back at me and I sport a short, and normally neatly trimmed, beard.

While I am not in the shape I was in when much younger and playing rugby and squash or later playing slow pitch and running ten K's, today my three or four rounds of golf a week, hiking when I can, and two or three dog walks per day keep me looking pretty fit. I think so anyway. At just under six feet tall, I still retain a 'fighting weight' of about 165 pounds.

Oddly, as a Canadian male with athletic aspirations, I didn't play hockey as a kid. As I said, our family was not wealthy, not even close, so we couldn't afford for me to play. Our mother went back to work when I was about 14 and that extra family income would have allowed me to finally get the required equipment to sign up. But a fourteen year old starting to play hockey in Canada, especially if they cannot skate well, would be like being a piñata at a birthday party comprised of obese kids each celebrating a sugar high. You would quite simply get pummelled.

Never being a guy for big breakfasts, after a coffee, a banana and a small bowl of whole wheat cereal, I direct my attention back to the document I received yesterday and my tentative plan.

On whisky tours to Islay and then Speyside in Scotland about ten years back my wife and I had the occasion to strike up a friendship with a history professor from Stanford University, Andrew (Andy) Hutchins, and his wife, Gill. Andy also has a reputation for being good at authenticating documents, something he picked up as part of his interest and expertise in American history. I experienced his skill first hand when he and I, and our wives, were exploring an old bookstore in Inverness while on our whisky tours.

Of similar age, we have become pretty good buddies and, despite the geographic distance between us, we usually find time for a face to face visit once or twice a year. We both like to go to spring training baseball in Scottsdale, both diehard Giants fans, and often meet up there to watch baseball and play golf.

As part of my plan in respect to the Lincoln document, I put in a call to him at Stanford. The call goes to voice mail where I hear a message that he is lecturing this morning. I briefly describe my dilemma and tell him I will scan and e-mail him a copy of the Lincoln document. I ask him to have a look and get back to me with any thoughts or opinions.

Message for Andy sent, I get on with the rest of my day, beginning with taking Jack for a long walk along by the waterfront near my place. Jack is happy, nose to the ground sniffing every new aroma that has arrived since yesterday's walk. I find the distraction of the walk welcome.

Em was always into horses so we have always lived in more rural areas, complete with barn, outdoor riding arenas and paddocks. When she died I couldn't find it in myself to move back into town proper. So I bought a nice three-bedroom home on a quarter-acre lot just a couple of hundred yards from the sea, a great place to walk the dog and for long walks on my own. The weather on Southern Vancouver Island can be pleasant all year round so being by the sea is a true privilege. Plus I can often golf fifty-two weeks a year.

It is not until the late afternoon that I hear back from Andy. He is quite animated on the phone and starts into a non-stop ramble almost before I can say hello.

"Jay, how the heck are you. It's been too long. I got your e-mail and read the attachment and then reread it and reread it. This is quite the document. Of course I cannot tell you if it is authentic or not. I would need to see the original and, even then, I don't have the expertise to be 100% sure. It is a real game changer if it is real. Do you understand the ramifications?"

Before I can say much in response he starts up again.

"Jay, I am not a lawyer or a high finance guy but the dollar implications of this are astronomical. The way this is worded, in today's dollars, and if I read this right these obligations would be in today's dollars, oh and plus interest, the dollar obligations are likely in the billions. That is just the easy part. If these lands were to be turned over to the 'lawfully declared" owners then what? This land now encompasses houses, schools, shopping malls, maybe even entire towns. This would be the biggest land transfer since the Louisiana Purchase."

"I know, Andy," I reply while I can finally sneak a word in.

"Jay, I did a bit of research and, at the start of the Civil War, there were almost 4 million slaves. Let's say one in five of those enslaved may have been deemed entitled to a land grant or land transfer, whatever it is called! We are talking millions of acres in the Carolinas, the Virginias, Maryland, Georgia, throughout the entire South. There were about a hundred thousand slaves in the North too. New Jersey and New Hampshire never banned slavery. It took the Emancipation Proclamation to do that. In point of fact it wasn't until 2020 that the words "Rhode Island and Providence Plantations" stopped appearing on Rhode Island's official state documents.

"Before the war some Southern states had a population base that was more than 50% enslaved people. These people's current relatives could claim half of some states, well maybe not half but huge swathes of land and money."

He added, "Think of the political fallout. Think of the social, economic, and cultural ramifications. Think, Jay, my God just think, about the racial connotations especially in the USA of today where the country seems so polarized already. People would be lined up on both sides of any debate and firing darts, or worse, at each other."

"Andy, I agree," I say when I finally get to speak. "I haven't slept well since I got this document in the courier. All these thoughts have been running through my mind as well. I am at a loss as to what to do about it, who to show it to or who give it to. It is all beyond me."

"Jay, if you ask me I would do nothing until you know that the document is real or has a chance of being real. If it is just a bit of fluff then you can do with it as you wish. Frame it and hang it on the wall or stick it in the round file. But, if it is real, well then that is another subject altogether.

"You need to get this into the hands of an expert, someone who can validate the document's age and signature. But, it will need to be an expert you can trust and one who can keep his or her mouth shut. If word of this gets out every wacko and crackpot south of your border will be gunning for you, not to mention every Mayor, Governor and politician in the Deep South. Thousands of folks will be lined up to embrace this while others will be lined up to stop it from becoming public or becoming policy."

"Yes and the lawyers would all be lined up for their fat fair share too," I added somewhat cynically.

"Agreed," replied Andy, "And if it is authentic, the current legal validity of it would also be a huge question. Supreme Court stuff! I am not certain if there is a best before date on Presidential Executive Orders.

"Given this was in a time of war Lincoln's presidential powers may have been extraordinary at that time as well. As for longevity, if memory serves, I actually think one Executive Order issued by Ulysses S. Grant is still valid today."

"Andy, I am off to the U.K. in two days, first London and then up to Alnmouth in Northumberland. It's too late to change my plans. Besides I do want to get away. So you and I will have to keep this under tight wraps until I get back."

"I have a better plan, Jay. I have a connection in London who is one of Europe's best at aging and determining the validity of old documents. I will text you his details. He has a shop on Charing Cross in the West End of London. Go in and see him when you are there. Show it to him. He should be able to determine authenticity. Also, he is very professional and can be trusted to keep this under wraps.

"One more thought, Jay. Gill frequently does some legal work for our old friend Senator Murchison, you know, the senior Senator from California. He has a real interest in past governmental indiscretions. Gill and I might have a quiet word with him tonight. We see him and his wife socially quite often. We are old school chums and, fortunately, tonight he is hosting a small gathering at his home. I will gently prod him on his thoughts without specifically mentioning the document or without giving too much away."

By way of expressing my agreement, I respond with, "Sounds like a plan, Andy. I will let you know how I make out in the U.K. and we can move on from there. Let me know what the Senator has to say. Talk soon and thanks for your advice and support and for always being there. You are a good friend despite you trouncing me too often in golf."

After my conversation with Andy I intend to spend the next day and a half working out final plans for my trip and trying to put the document out of my mind, at least until London.

3

That night, Andy, and his wife, Gill, enjoy dinner at the palatial home of Senator Thomas Jefferson Murchison. Small of statue, but with a commanding presences, Senator Murchison is a three term Senator for California. He is articulate, polished, determined and even ruthless when required. He is also, like most good politicians, extremely pragmatic.

He is known to be left of left on most issues. He is particularly focussed on racial disparity issues in the US and has consistently lobbied for minority rights. In fact he has long been urging the sitting President to formally and finally give a Presidential apology to the ancestors of slaves. Apparently this has never been done formally by any President.

Murchison is also expected to be his Party's nominee in the next Presidential election.

This small dinner party includes, among others, 5 friends from University days at Stanford. The Senator met his wife there while he was studying law. His stunningly beautiful wife, Jennifer, was busy studying the best prospects for a rich husband and seems to have graduated with honours.

Andy also met his wife there. He of course was studying History and Gill, his wife, was, like the Senator, studying Law. Also stunningly beautiful and very much focussed on the world outside their home she has a successful law practice in San Francisco. Much of her time these days is aimed at not-for-profits and pro bono work. Both Andy and Gill are fitness freaks whose appearance belies they are both in their early 50's. As committed as they are to fitness, both are equally active in community affairs and keen observers of world affairs.

Gill and the Senator's wife, Jennifer, were best friends even before University. They grew up together in Sausalito and have been pals since they met in first grade.

The fifth Stanford University friend is a wealthy neighbour and very close friend of all the other alumni, Bill Murphy. Not just a neighbour and University friend, Bill has also been a very significant contributor to all of the Senator's campaigns.

Large, even rotund, likely due to his proclivity for sixteen ounce Porterhouse steaks, fully loaded baked potatoes and decadent desserts, Murphy is a gregarious and fun loving man who proudly pronounces that he enjoys only the simple things in life as long as they are also the best... the best food, the best wine, the best homes (he has several) and the best cars. Despite his fondness for the finest of things he is also generous to a fault and a loyal and trusted friend.

His wife, actually second wife, Suzanne, is some 15 years younger than all the Stanford alumni around the table and seems to have more interest during dinner in the seventh member of the dinner party than of the other five. His name is Ian Ralston and he is the recently hired Communications Director for the Senator and is presumably in line to be his Campaign Manager once the expected Presidential run is formally announced by Murchison.

Ralston, about the same age as Murphy's wife, is a very impressive young man. Impeccably dressed and impeccably presented, extremely articulate in both speech and conduct, quick with a quip or intelligent comment, his potential would seem to be limitless. As, seemingly, would be his potential to attract young female admirers, single or not. He is handsome, fit, and known to be exceedingly ambitious.

Murphy and the Senator had both made obscene amounts of money in the late 1990s in the burgeoning tech Industry in California. The Senator uses his gobs of money to try and change the political landscape by moving it to the Left. Murphy uses his gobs of money to support good causes everywhere, most of them of the socially conscience variety. He also owns a very prestigious winery up at Napa which he spent millions developing. This winery is his pride and joy. The rest of his generous financial resources seem to be aimed at keeping his young wife in jewelry, high fashion, and a myriad of good-looking male tennis coaches.

Dinner is a sometimes raucous affair spent revisiting University days, Fraternity and Sorority parties, protest marches, favorite classes, favorite professors, favorite hangouts, and favourite songs. Suzanne and Ralston contribute when they can, which is seldom when competing with the 5 old Stanford friends. Copious amounts of Bill Murphy's best Cabernet Sauvignon, currently going at $100 a bottle at the winery in Napa, is enjoyed by all.

After dinner, and in a very old fashioned way, the men adjourn to the study while the women stay chatting around the dining room table.

Once all are settled in the Senator's study, Andy eases into the topic discussed with Jay by offering, "Anyone know much about the history of Presidential Executive Orders?"

Senator Murchison replies, "Andy, I thought you were the expert."

"Not when it comes to political issues, Jefferson. Whoops I mean Senator," He adds with a mischievous grin. "All of us Neanderthals leave the politics up to you."

"Ha ha, very funny, but why do you ask, Andy?"

"An old friend asked me to look into it Senator. Evidently he is curious about the circumstances under which one is brought into law, the power they hold, over whom, how long they are in effect for, and how or when they can be overridden."

"That's quite a list, Andy. What I can tell you is these Orders are infrequent but not rare. They are supposed to be directives from a President to help manage the operations of the government. The vast majority of executive orders are actually proposed by federal agencies and recommended to the President.

"While not actually enshrined in the Constitution, Article Two of the Constitution grants Presidents broad executive and enforcement authority to use their discretion to determine how to enforce the law or to otherwise manage the resources and staff of the executive branch.

"If memory serves, the first Executive Order was issued by Washington around 1789. Without doubt the most famous Executive Order was from Lincoln when he issued the Emancipation Proclamation in 1863. To show the range of jurisdiction that can be impacted, the Emancipation Proclamation contained explicit directions to the Army, the Navy, as well as to other Executive departments.

"Until the early 1900s, Executive Orders were mostly unannounced and undocumented and most often seen only by the agencies to which they were directed. The Department of State finally instituted a numbering scheme in 1907 and this numbering was done retroactively right back to Washington's first one in1789.

"As for longevity, I believe one issued by U.S. Grant is still valid today. But, for the life of me, I cannot remember what it is or was about.

"To answer your last question, Andy, a President can cancel, revoke, modify or make exceptions from any Executive Order, whether the Order was made by the current President or a predecessor."

"Thanks for this, Senator. I knew you would be a wealth of knowledge on the topic," Andy replied.

Looking inquisitively the Senator asks, "Why the interest, Andy?"

"Oddly I was in a conversation the other day with an old friend who was asking. He was just speculating about a scenario where an Executive Order may have been issued but for some reason was never actioned because of Presidential illness or other overriding circumstances. He was asking me, if such an Order existed, would it still be valid if this oversight came to light today."

Ian Ralston, the newly hired Communications Director pipes in, "This is still pretty vague, Andy. Can you be a bit more specific as to what the question really is? I don't want the Senator to get into trouble by speculating on something this vague. Not that you would drop the Senator in the glue but I have to do my job," he adds with a self-assured, almost arrogant smile.

Despite his promise to me to only gently prod the Senator, Andy offers, "With a lot of talk lately from the Southern Baptist Coalition about reparations for the families of those formerly enslaved, suppose Lincoln had issued an Executive Order detailing specific reparations but, because of his sudden death, this Order did not get actioned, even though it was legally issued and hence could still be legally binding?"

"Well," says the Senator, looking perplexed, "That would present a political and cultural hurricane not seen in many years. You do have a great imagination, Andy," he adds anxiously, "Or is it just imagination?"

"Yes, do you know something we don't know, Andy?" Ian Ralston interjects rather pointedly.

"No. Just trying to respond to a question my Canadian buddy who lives up near Victoria was asking of me. He has an over-zealous imagination just like too many of the students in my classes these days. He is also an old history buff. I thought it was an interesting proposition and thought it would offer some fun to toss it about. Not to change the subject but do you have any more of that good Scotch, Senator?"

Despite a rather distressed look from Ian Ralston, with that segue so skillfully orchestrated by Andy, the conversation returns to more mundane issues.

An hour or so later, while the Senator and his wife are saying goodnight to Andy, Ian Ralston approaches Andy's wife, Gill.

"Gill, what is Andy's friend's name, the one up in British Columbia? I was thinking about heading up that way this summer to have a look around and it might be kind of nice to chat with someone from up there about what to do and see. And, as he is a friend of Andy's, I am sure he would be a great connection."

"His name is Jay Alexander. I will text you his contact information. No sense rushing to talk with him though as I am pretty sure Andy said that Jay flies to London Heathrow the day after tomorrow. He goes to London for a few days a couple of times a year and then heads up to Northumberland, Alnmouth I believe, to play golf and walk the beaches there. I think it helps him deal with the tragic loss of his wife."

"Oh, I am so sorry to hear about his wife. But, thanks for this Gill. I look forward to getting Jay Alexander's contact info. It was lovely to meet you. I look so forward to working with the Senator and with you, he adds somewhat suggestively. I also look forward to connecting with Andy's friend but I'll wait for a month or so to give him time to complete his trip and get settled back at home. Goodnight now."

Ralston leaves, but only after giving Gill a kiss on the cheek rather than the more traditionally expected handshake.

When Ian Ralston gets into his car, after the all the formal goodbyes, he reaches for his cell phone, not the office phone but a newly acquired burner phone. He always seems to have one of these burner phones with him. He quickly dials a number from memory.

The call he makes is to Tyrone Thorn, an important conduit and leader in an ultra-right organization called the Freedom Brotherhood. Thorn is a smart and determined man with a Military background, having served two tours of duty in the Middle-East. He is an ROTC graduate and hence served there as an officer. He left the armed forces under a bit of a cloud after an investigation concerning the poor treatment of locals in the military zones where he was serving. A few other officers and enlisted men serving under him there at the time left under the same cloud.

Some of the rumours about his conduct were downright alarming. He elected, or perhaps was nudged, to leave voluntarily once his eight years of compulsory ROTC service expired.

An engineer by profession, and by all accounts once a good one, most of his time is now spent in organizing and lobbying for fringe causes on the far Right. How he is compensated is not clear. Rumours abound about drugs or weapons changing hands or backdoor secret donations.

As the call from Ralston comes through, Thorn picks up the phone almost immediately and after simply saying hello, he hears Ralston speak.

"Tyrone, we may have a problem."

"Ian, first contact since we got you ensconced in the job with that wacko Woke Senator from California. And, now you say we already have a problem? That's fast. So, what's the problem?"

"You know all this chatter lately from the Southern Baptist Coalition about some sort of compensation or restitution for the families of former slaves, a big bunch of liberal mollycoddling. Anyway at dinner at the Senator's tonight one of his guests was asking a poorly veiled question about a possible Executive Order from Lincoln that committed the Country to reparations."

"Ian, Lincoln has been dead for 150 years. What's the worry?"

"Executive Orders apparently don't expire and I get a sense there is some kind of proof that such an Order exists. We need to find out if it does exist and, if it exists, kill it before it becomes public and hence of major concern."

"Do you think this guest has this proof?"

"No, Tyrone, but the key is a Canadian named Jay Alexander. He is the guy that really posed the question via the Senator's guest. This Jay Alexander character is flying from Vancouver to London Heathrow in two days. I suggest you get someone on his flight and track him to see what he is up to. Maybe a quiet chat with him might shake out the truth or, if needed, maybe a really loud shake might quiet the truth."

"Yeah, maybe, but just remember, Ian, you work for me not the other way round. I make the suggestions, remember. Anyway, good work and a good idea. I will make sure I get someone on that plane.

"And Ian, we need to keep in touch on this. Let me know if that wack job Senator has any other interesting info to divulge. That's what you were put there for. And keep your head down. We don't want anyone to find out that the Brothers of Freedom have another Senator in our pocket, even if this one doesn't know we own him yet."

Immediately after hanging up with Ian Ralston, Tyrone puts a call into Senator Layton Conrad. Senator Conrad was Ralston's former boss and it is he who managed, rather deviously, to maneuver Ralston into the employ of his would be political enemy, Senator Murchison of California.

Senator Conrad, like his political rival Senator Murchison, is also short of stature. Thin, balding but surprisingly still physically imposing, he is quite a bit older than his rival. He is also known to be even more determined and even more ruthless when the occasion arises or when it suits his fancy. Most who know him would call him a bully. He apparently has no life to speak of outside the realm of politics. He is a powerful figure in his Party and has already begun a campaign to become his Party's candidate in the upcoming Presidential election, just a little over one year hence. He is known to stop at nothing to get whatever it is he wants and to squash anyone who stands in his way. If you were to look up the word 'ruthless' in the dictionary you would likely see Senator Conrad's photo there beside the definition.

Conrad answers the phone and hears, "Senator, it's me, Tyrone, and yes, the call is safe. I need to let you know that we may have a problem. Ian just called me after a surprise was dropped on him during dinner at Murchison's tonight. While it is not 100% certain, it seems that there may be some type of old legal document that has just emerged, believe it or not from Abraham Lincoln himself, that promises major restitution to former slaves.

"If it is true, this Lincoln promise could see great swaths of land forcibly change hands in the South, not to mention billions of dollars going to blacks down there. Your constituents would go nuts, not to mention how this flies in the face of everything we have been working to preserve and protect in the midst of all this Woke bull shit. First it's the Confederate flag. Then it's statues of Robert E. Lee. Now we may be talking about ripping land out of the hands of good God-fearing folks and gifting it to the shiftless, the druggies and the rest. Fuck me Senator, this can't happen."

"You say you are not sure, Tyrone. What are the odds this document exists?"

"Still trying to find out for certain but I am sending Gunnar and Wyatt to London to try and follow the trail. It starts with some Canadian named Jay Alexander. This Alexander guy is flying to London in two days and may have the document with him. I will have Gunnar and Wyatt put eyes and ears on him and, if opportunity presents, they will grab the document and make sure it never sees the light of day."

"Shit, Tyrone, this doesn't sound good. Keep me informed and also keep an eye on those two you are going to send over. I know they are committed to our position but, muscles notwithstanding, between them those two have a combined IQ of about eleven. That's why they were both bounced from the Army."

"Will do Senator."

"In the meantime I will think this through and maybe plant a false flag or two that can head this off no matter what those two morons accomplish. I always have a few good media contacts that owe me. It is time to call in a favour or two. I just might be able to start the rumour mill in motion before anyone else gets wind of this."

Conversation over, both hang-up and both are left to contemplate their next steps to bring this matter to a satisfactory resolve for the 'Brotherhood.'

4

Day Three

Keeping with his commitment to Senator Conrad, Tyrone Thorn gets up early the next morning and immediately completes a number of hurry up travel arrangements. Once done, he puts in a call to his former military brother in arms, and current Brotherhood comrade, Gunnar Nielson. Nielsen answers on the first ring.

"Gunnar, it is me, Tyrone. We may have a problem." He then fully briefs Gunnar Nielsen on the situation concerning the possible Lincoln promise.

After providing a thorough briefing he adds, "We need you and Wyatt on an Air Canada flight tomorrow out of Vancouver, B.C. This is a direct flight to London Heathrow. We need you to track a Canadian by the name of Jay Alexander. He will be on that flight. He apparently has some kind information or proof with him about this Lincoln issue.

"The flight leaves Vancouver at 18.40 tomorrow. I have booked seats for you both. I have also booked a hotel for you for 2 nights in London. You can extend that booking if you need to, once there. I will text you all the details and the tickets after this call. Got that?"

"Shit, Tyrone, we are Coeur d'Alene. Vancouver is a long ways from here."

"I know. I checked distances before I phoned. It has to be you two as no one else can get there in time. It is about a 7-hour drive from Coeur d'Alene to Vancouver. We need eyes and ears on this Jay Alexander guy ASAP. You two are going to have to drive up to Vancouver in time to catch that flight. You have the rest of today and most of tomorrow to do so. Just make sure you are on that plane and tracking this guy."

"Easier said than done, Tyrone! The drive is one thing but what does this guy look like? How do we find him on a flight of 350 plus people? Vancouver airport isn't small and Heathrow airport is a hell of a lot bigger than that."

"That is for you to figure out Gunnar. Use your imagination. I don't know? Page the bastard at check-in. Tell the check-in desk some tale of woe. Whatever! Anyway, get on with it. I need you to find this Alexander guy, get hold of whatever it is he has with him, and see that it disappears forever. Do whatever it takes Gunnar. Whatever it takes! Now you better get going. You will need to fill in Wyatt as soon as you can and start out for Vancouver. Keep me informed and don't screw it up. This is very, very important."

Thorn continues, "Buy a couple of phones once you get there and then make contact with me right away so I will be able to reach you both if necessary."

Instructions delivered, Thorn abruptly ends the call and gets on with dispatching the tickets and travel details to his two accomplices. He is hoping all will be fine but has a nagging feeling to the contrary.

After the excitement of finding the box and sharing its big surprising contents with Andy yesterday, I spend much of today packing and taking care of all the little things one needs to do before heading away for a couple of weeks.

I arrange for someone to pick up my newspaper. I still get the *Globe and Mail* delivered daily. I know this is old fashioned but I cannot get used to reading Op-Eds and well-written political columns on-line. I need my daily fix of newsprint. You can't change a thirty plus year habit overnight.

As a former Senior Federal Public Servant I still hold a keen interest in Canadian and International political issues. I have a particularly keen interest in what has been going on in Eastern Europe and stateside over the last several years. *The Globe* helps keep me up to date and I trust it much more than most of those wanna-be online news sources.

Things seem to be becoming more and more polarized in Europe and down south. In my humble view some of the 'Western World's' great democracy seems to have forgotten what democracy actually is. Enough said. I certainly don't want to offend anyone, but things look a bit bleak if I can be brutally honest.

Going from the global to the very, very local, other chores to attend to before I leave include taking out the compost bucket from under the sink and depositing it outside in the big compost bin. I turn off the hot water heater and empty the fridge of anything that would/might spoil. I would arrange for someone to come in and water my plants but apparently plastic plants don't need watering.

I contemplate a quick 9 holes of golf but my clubs have already been dispatched overseas. They are currently travelling business class as compared to the premium economy seat I booked.

Finally I check with my neighbours to make sure they have everything they need to take care of Jack while I am away; water dish, food dish, leash, a few of his favorite toys, his comfortable bed, and the three types of ridiculously expensive food he gets mixed together for his twice a day meals. The dog eats better than I do.

I arrange for the time I will drop Jack, and all this paraphernalia, off in the morning. I then take Jack for a walk and spend the rest of the day in fairly quiet reflection about my holiday plans, about the state of my love life and, most worryingly, about the document I got by courier two days ago.

Day Four

I am up early even though the first leg of my flight is hours away. I always get keyed up before a long flight. Not sure why, but I do. And, of course, this time I have a reason to be keyed up. Shortly after noon I drop off Jack and say my good byes to my neighbours. Jack is too distracted by the neighbours' cat to see me heading out the door. He will miss me later, of that I am sure

After a brief thirty-minute hop by plane from Victoria to Vancouver I face a three-and-a-half-hour wait at the Vancouver International Terminal before I am off non-stop to Heathrow. Even though I can afford it, and unlike my golf clubs mode of travel, I am too cheap to fly business class. I do splurge for Premium Economy however as I appreciate the extra room. As I never sleep on the plane I often (and did this time) book my London hotel for the previous night so I can check straight in when I get into London proper in the morning.

One of my favorite things to do while waiting at airports is to observe other passengers in the waiting area and then build imaginary stories about them.

Over there in the grey pant suit, topped off with a red beret, is a Grandma going to see her new grandson for the first time. You can tell how excited she is by her pacing and her occasionally breaking into wide grins. She is carrying a package loaded with gifts for the youngster. I am surprised I cannot see knitting needles poking out of her bag. But I suppose airport security might frown on knitting needles on a flight.

That fellow with the heavy bags under his eyes, and a light carry-on, is a business man, too long in Canada. Business must not have been good. He looks beat, like he just wants to get home and see his wife and kids. Rather, in truth, it is more likely all he really wants is his own bed and ten hours of catch up sleep. Maybe he can do some catch up on the plane, but unlikely in a full flight, while sitting in economy. The heavy bags under his eyes are because he was too long at the bar last night. Another of the walking wounded of international commerce.

That woman in the off the shoulder dress, wearing too much makeup, and showing too much cleavage (if there is such a thing) is named 'Victoria' and she has a Secret. She is off for a clandestine meeting with a lover who she secretly meets up with at least once a year, always after feigning a required visit to a sick aunt in Coventry. The affair I imagine has been going on for years. Apparently her aunt gets sick quite often. She may or may not be leaving an adoring husband at home. The way she carries herself she is either amorously anxious or else she just has gas.

Those two playing footsies and making eyes at each other are off on a second honeymoon and have already started to get in the mood. They are leaving all their home worries – mortgage, kids, medical bills etc. behind them. Judging from the way they are dressed the destination is somewhere warm. Therefore London cannot be their final stop. Likely Greece, Portugal or southern Spain. Lucky buggers! It would be nice to be heading somewhere warm with someone you love. Heck, it would be nice to have someone to love.

Those two muscle bound guys, with the shaved heads and 'one too many' tattoos, are off to London for a second rate Mr. Universe contest or an Over the Top Battle Royal. One of them seems to be pretty proud of coming from Idaho judging from the patches on his jacket. Why fly out of Vancouver however? The other one, the shorter of the two, just seems to be proud of his biceps. It is as if someone cloned the larger one and replicated him in one of those 3-D printers set for ¾ actual size. I hope one of them is not sitting next to me. Premium economy seats are larger but not if you are sharing a row with one of those two behemoths.

Does anyone else look around an airport waiting area and guess who is going to be sitting beside you on the flight? I do this all the time too and I particularly single out those that I definitely ***do not want*** sitting beside me. Is she pretty? Well then okay. Not pretty, maybe not. Overweight, definitely out. Too young? Too old? Too chatty? Too sullen? Too much carry-on with them to fit easily into the overhead. Odd food smell? Snores? Cries? Laughs too much? Picky, picky. I suppose I am just a snob at heart.

I bet you could learn a lot about a person just by analyzing the choices they might make about a would-be seat mate on a long flight. I wonder if that is part of the Myers-Briggs assessment. If not, it should be!

I do have a seriously over active imagination but it is fun and helps pass time. Perhaps I need a new hobby or maybe I need to take up writing fantasy novels.

To my surprise, about forty minutes before boarding, I hear a page, "Mr. Alexander, please report to the check-in desk for an important message."

Intrigued, I rush up to the desk, inform the women at the desk that I am Mr. Alexander, and enquire about the message. The woman at the desk gives me a pleasant smile and then hands me an envelope with my name written on it.

I quickly open the envelope and written inside, on a piece of torn paper, is a single word, "Hello."

Mystified, I ask her who gave her the message. She tells me an older gentleman approached and told her he was asked to drop the envelope off and that he had been told it was important. She adds he told her that he was doing this at the request of someone who had to hurry off to catch a flight and needed his help urgently. He didn't describe the person who gave him the envelope and I never asked. As he said it was important I paged you immediately.

I thank her and return to where I was sitting before hearing the page. There I sit in stunned silence, thinking what the hell is that all about? A secret admirer? Maybe the lady with the exposed cleavage? There I go again with my imagination.

Finally, boarding is announced and my mind turns to more important things like finding my seat and passing judgement on my seat mate. Boarding completed, off we go and my U.K. adventure begins. My happy thoughts about a nice break are mixed with trepidation and doubt.

Day Five

After a restless night on the plane, and three mediocre movies to help pass the time, I arrive at 10.30 the next morning at Heathrow. After a race through the Heathrow maze, I hop on the Heathrow Express to Paddington Station and am walking toward my Hotel not much more than forty-five minutes after touch down.

The new Visas and Immigration process at Heathrow is so quick now that you are well clear of there before your luggage gets to the carousel. Less than five years ago this was the reverse. It took forever to get through Immigration so your luggage was usually waiting for you by that time.

Funny story, a few years back I got a luggage tag from Em in my Christmas stocking that said, "Put this bag back it isn't yours." On my next U.K. visit, when I finally got through immigration, my bag was there but someone had stolen the luggage tag. Some people's children! But pretty funny in retrospect. One of these days I will see that tag on a carousel and will snag it. All's fair in love, war, and baggage tag theft.

Upon leaving the Heathrow Express train, I walk the few blocks from Paddington Station to my Hotel on Sussex Gardens. There is a light rain shower so I take the pack light jacket from the backpack I always travel with and put the jacket on. I add a ball cap, from Barbour no less. It is not raining hard enough to make me haul out my folding umbrella. I always travel light so I just need to pull a small wheeled suitcase behind me.

No need to tote my golf clubs. They have long since been gone having travelled on their own directly to Alnmouth with one of those companies that will ship your clubs to where ever you want for exactly the same price it would cost for a new set once you get there.

I am glad I booked and paid for the previous night at the Hotel as I am able to get right into my room without having to wait for the standard 3.00pm check-in time.

Perhaps odd to some, but as often as I am in the U.K. the first time I cross a street, upon arriving in London, it always hits me about the direction the traffic is flowing in. It is so counter intuitive when coming from North America. Here the saying, "Look both ways before you cross," has extra important meaning. I am always cautious crossing U.K. roads. Did I mention I would never drive over here, not in London, not anywhere in the U.K. in fact?

I have always had an aversion to too much fuss when travelling so I always stay at the same small three star hotel in Paddington when they have a room available. Even when travelling with the Government, during all my years with them, and having my expenses covered, I avoided the big fancy chain hotels.

I do not like all that fuss during check-in at those big name properties. I can find my own room thank you and I don't need anyone to carry up my luggage for me. When I do I will likely be too old to travel anyway.

I know the Paddington and Bayswater areas well, the pubs, the restaurants, the tube stations, and can walk or easily take the tube to just about everyplace I need. Also, I only stay in London for a few days on each of my trips before heading off somewhere else, so I don't need to be able to wander too far afield.

After checking in at the hotel and going straight up to my room to drop off my luggage I head back to Paddington Station to buy my train ticket for Alnmouth. Once bought I walk through the station and up past the taxi rank to grab a coffee and a light lunch at one of those floating narrowboats in Little Venice. This is one of my favorite quiet spots in this big, busy city.

Small world as, while walking from the hotel, I see those shaved headed wrestlers, let's call them Mr. Clean look alikes, I saw at the Vancouver airport. They are standing on Sussex Gardens consulting a map. Likely trying to find the closest Gym, steroid outlet or

Mr. Big and Broad clothing store. I always wonder why guys want to pump so much iron that their arms can never actually touch their sides. Their arms just sort of float out there on a 30 degree angle. Guess maybe I am just jealous, hah!

After my light lunch on a narrow boat restaurant I go back to my room, fetch the Lincoln document, and take the tube from Lancaster Gate to Tottenham Court. Once off the tube I walk a few blocks down Charing Cross to talk with the expert my friend, Andy, had recommended I go see.

When I get to 'Vintage Maps and Books' on Charing Cross I pop in and talk to a young, casually dressed, fellow behind the counter. His name tag says his name is John and he looks to be about 15 judging from the peach fuzz on his chin. I ask to speak with Andy's contact by name. The young fellow tells me that his boss, Milton, the expert I came to see, has been off ill for several months, and without me asking, adds that the illness is quite serious. He then asks me what I wanted to talk about and asks if he can help.

I tell him I have a document that may have come from President Lincoln and I wanted to see if someone could help me verify its authenticity, or lack there-of. He is very emphatic that he cannot help me but suggests someone in a vintage book store on Portobello Road and gives me the name and address. He does offer to sell me some books on Lincoln but I politely decline.

I head out and grab the tube to Notting Hill Gate. It is just four or five stops along the Central Line on the tube from Tottenham Court. Funny, but there again I see the two 'Mister Cleans' wandering down Charing Cross toward me. Eerily it almost seems like I am being stalked by these two goons but I calm myself by remembering I have always had an overly creative imagination.

Unbeknownst to me, these two 'Mister Cleans' head to the same book store I just came out of. After a few words with this same young fellow behind the counter, and not getting the answers they want, the shorter of the two wanders back to the door and reverses the door sign to display closed instead of open. The two then re-approach the clerk to question him in more detail.

I get off the tube at Notting Hill Gate and wander past all the second hand stores on my way down to Portobello Road. Once there I find the book shop I am looking for, about half way down the famous market street. The book store is open but I am told by the proprietor that the expert I am looking for is only in on Saturdays, the busiest day of the week at the famous Portobello (Notting Hill) Market. Hugh Grant, Julia Roberts and a little blue travel book shop anyone?

While chatting with the proprietor I remember that one of the best book stores in the world, and one well versed in vintage documents, is in Alnwick. Alnwick is just a few miles from where I will be the day after tomorrow. I thank the proprietor and, as I am leaving, remark that I will check with the book store in Alnwick, as I will be in Alnmouth in just two days. He replies that he knows of that book store and of its outstanding reputation for authenticating documents. He wishes me luck and off I go.

I hop back on the tube at Notting Hill Gate station, get off at Lancaster Gate, and head to my favorite local pub. It is just a stone's throw from the tube stop and from my hotel. Interestingly the pub has the same name as the hotel I am staying at but they are not affiliated.

When I walk into any English pub I always try and order a pint of ale I am unfamiliar with. I always check the names on the taps to see what is new, or at least, what is new to me. If you ask the barman nicely they will usually pour you a small sample to try. You never know when you will find the perfect pint and, besides, life is too short to only drink one brand of ale.

I taste three ales gratis and order the one I like best of the three I sampled. I add a pack of crisps and a pack of Nobby's Nuts as a snack. I ask for regular flavoured crisps. Who in their right mind would want to eat prawn flavoured crisps? Haggis flavoured crisps? Yuck!

I take a table for two by the window and sit down, my back to the wall, to relax and gather my thoughts. My head is awash with visions ranging from golf, to beach walks, to 150-year-old documents, to bald headed wrestlers.

Finally, after my brief respite at the pub, I'm off back to the hotel for a few hours rest before I venture out for dinner. It is just a few blocks walk. It has been a busy day and I got almost no sleep on the flight and I am very tired. I do have one travel rule about jet lag however. I never nap on the first day no matter how tired I am. I steadfastly stay awake until the normal bed time at the new location. This allows the time adjustment to work much more quickly and effectively. Well, it works for me, anyway.

The hotel I stay at always asks that you leave the key at the desk when leaving and you ask for it again when you return. The front desk clerk looks at me rather oddly when I ask for the key to room 304. In fact she asks if I am sure that is my room number. Once I assure her that 304 is indeed my room number, and she confirms my name is what is on the reservation for 304, she hands me the key.

When I get to the room it is obvious someone else has been in it. My suitcase has been emptied and is upside down on the floor. The bed has been tossed and my toiletry case has been tipped onto the bed. While nothing seems to be missing I am none-the-less annoyed and dismayed. This is the last thing I expected or needed.

Not waiting for the elevator, I run straight back down the 3 flights of narrow stairs leading to the front desk to find out what the hell has been going on. The same clerk is there at the front desk. When I ask about my room she tells me that my roommate had been in an hour or so earlier and had asked for the key.

In a very puzzled way, I enquire of her, "My roommate?"

She replies, "Yeah, the stout fellow with the shaved head. He said his name was Jay Alexander, and wanted the key but, as he had just checked in this morning and was very tired, he couldn't remember the room number. I checked and Mr. Alexander was the name of the registered guest in 304 so I gave him the key."

I inform her that whoever was in the room earlier was not me and was not there with my permission. I then reconfirm I am who I say I am by showing her my passport and other photo ID. I ask her to ensure no one else gets into the room besides me. I also ask her to be sure she informs the night staff and tomorrow's day staff about this.

That said, I next ask for a key to a hotel courtesy security box. These boxes are conveniently located in a room just off of, but in clear site of, the hotel front desk. Much better than those little security boxes most hotels leave on the bottom shelf of closets in their rooms. You have to lie flat on the floor to read the instructions and put in a code to open or lock one of those boxes. Try that without reading glasses. I cannot image being seventy years old and trying to use one of those things.

I immediately remove from my backpack the Lincoln document, my passport, and some extra English pounds I usually carry when in the U.K. I then lock them all in the security box. I am assured there is only one key per box and that I now have it. The clerk reminds me, rather sternly, it is the only key and not to lose it. Somehow I have the feeling that she thinks it is my fault someone got into my room, not hers.

Documents and money now secured, I have to think further on my room being tossed. I am more than just a little suspicious. In fact I am quite worried. Something is going on. Given the description the desk clerk gave of the pretend Mr. Alexander it seems obvious to me who has been in my room, or has my imagination gone wild again?

It must be those two goons I keep running into. If those two toughs, I now refer to them in my mind as 'Clean and Jerk,' are following me then I am glad I am out of London the day after tomorrow. But I also wonder how they would even know I am in

London let alone that I might have a document of some importance. I vow to call Andy later, remembering the eight hour time difference between London and California, to see if he has told anyone about my mission.

I grab a light gammon steak supper at another favoured pub just down the road, wash it down with a pint or two of IPA and head back to the hotel. Actually I had three pints but don't judge me as I have a lot on my mind and ale helps me think and to sleep as well, I hope.

There is a new person at the front desk and fortunately the new person is Rosa, a lovely young Spanish woman who knows me well. I have stayed at this hotel often over the years. She has worked there for all 10 years I have been coming here.

After saying our hellos and catching up briefly on our families, our health, and our well-being she informs me that the day clerk had told her about the room mix-up earlier.

She then tells me that a man had come in an hour or so ago, saying he was Mr. Alexander, and asking for the key to room 304.

She says, "Theese man came in and said he was Meester Alejander and asked for the key to room 304. I tell heem that I know Mr. Alejander very well and that he was indeed not Mr. Alejander. I tell heem I cannot help heem. He then was very rude and call me an eefing C word and he storm out of the hotel."

When I ask her to describe the man she says; "Very large man, with a beeg tattoo on his neck. I theenk it was a swastika. He have no hair on hees head. He is dressed in a two tone athlete's jacket and black pants. Very tall, very wide and looking very mean."

I enquire if he had an accent and she replied, "Yes, he talk very slow like they do on those American movies, you know, like Texas or Oklahoma or maybe not quite that slow. I don't know! One of those American places I theenk."

I thank Rosa and I tell her she did the right thing. She is such a lovely young woman. Always a pleasure to see and talk with. She is one of the many wonderful people I have met on my frequent travels over the last several years. To me travel is an essential in life if you want to really understand people and culture. And, if you are willing to engage and get a bit uncomfortable you will meet some very special folks where ever you go. In many, many ways I am an extreme introvert and so I know about getting uncomfortable in order to engage.

My conversation with Rosa over, I remind myself that I am thankful I put the document in the hotel security boxes to which, I had sternly been assured, I have the only key. I then head up to my room to call Andy, head swimming with questions and conspiracy scenarios.

I make my call to California and Andy picks up on the second ring. He informs me he is having lunch in his campus office and on an hour's break from his next class.

I explain the strange occurrences concerning Clean and Jerk and with my hotel room over the last two days. I remind him that he and I are the only two people who know about the document.

He fills me in on his full conversation with Senator Murchison and apologizes if he was a bit too forthcoming when discussing the issue with the Senator. He assures me that the Senator would have no issue with such a document becoming widely known and even actioned if it were confirmed to be authentic. He says the Senator has always been in favour of long overdue reparations.

To further illustrate, he explains how just last week the Senator took serious issue with the current Senate Majority Leader, Wilson Franks. Senate Majority Leader Franks recently affirmed to the media that, in essence, he didn't think reparations or apologies for something that happened 150 years ago are a good idea. Notably, he (Senate Majority Leader Franks) added, "Especially when none of us currently living are responsible for what happened back then."

"If that is how Senator Murchison feels," I responded, "It doesn't make any sense that he would take umbrage with my attempts to authentic the document. But why would two guys, assumedly Americans, be following me around London from book store to book store, and searching my hotel room, if the Senator is to be trusted. Did you tell anyone else, Andy?"

"Yes, I recall that I did. Included in my conversation with the Senator was his new Communications guy, a fellow named Ian Ralston. Ralston was also in the room when I broached the subject."

"Would he have spilled the beans, Andy?"

"I don't know much about him. The Senator just hired him. He told me he picked Ian Ralston because of his (Ralston's) avid disgust of the Senator he had worked for previously, Layton Conrad.

"Ralston's former boss, Layton Conrad, is a devious and clever bugger. His public image, rumours have it, belie his apparent connection with the ultra-right and, even more sinisterly, with a white supremacist paramilitary group called the Brothers of Freedom. In case you haven't heard these 'Brothers' operate under what they call the 4 F's, America 'first,' 'freedom' for all, 'foreigners' forbidden, and 'ferocity' against our enemies. Scary dudes one and all. To put this into perspective, this Conrad is rumoured to have said that the 1921 Tulsa race riots were a good start."

"Hmm", I add with disgust, "Sounds like a group of fine gentlemen. I can see why Ralston would want to quit this guy Conrad. But, do you think maybe this Ralston guy has a big mouth or let this slip somehow? You know how people almost always need to tell someone they have a secret. It makes them feel important. It seems apparent to me that someone talked with someone about this document. Somebody let the cat out of the bag. See if you can find anything more about Ralston and let me know, and Andy, let's not let anyone else know about this for now, please! I already feel threatened enough."

I sign off by telling Andy that I intend to continue with my vacation as well as my search for authentication but that I also intend to keep as low a profile as I can. I thank him in advance for following up on Ian Ralston and promise to keep him informed of my progress.

With that done, I phone back to Canada to check on Jack. He doesn't answer but I hear him in the background announcing his presence. I am assured he is fine. I next text the kids letting them know I have safely arrived and ask if there is anything the grandkids might like me to bring back. Text sent I head out to a highly touted whisky bar a few blocks away for a nice single malt nightcap. Am I drinking too much? I think not.

The pub culture in the U.K. is part of the charm of living and visiting here and whisky, like ale, helps me think. I have met some wonderful people in pubs over here. Many of them have become good friends.

After a nice night cap, Oban 14, I walk back to the hotel and my well-earned bed, albeit anticipating a night of tossing, turning and theorizing. And that is just what I get.

5

Day Six

Most of my second day in London turns out to be uneventful. I rise at about 8.00am, still a bit groggy given my jetlag, too much of the expected tossing and turning, and the eight hour time difference. I enjoy what the Hotel refers to as a 'Full English Breakfast.' It is actually on the rather small side, one egg, one rasher of bacon, a splash of beans and toast, but is provided gratis at the Hotel. I have never been a big breakfast guy anyway, but when in Rome.

After breakfast I go for a walk to the near-by Kensington Gardens. I then decide to really stretch my legs by walking all the way down through Hyde Park and along by Green Park to Leicester Square. My destination there is the 'day of' Leicester Square theatre ticket box office. After about a ten minute wait in line at the ticket booth I buy a ticket for that evening's performance of 'Come from Away.' It is a wonderful show about the citizens of Gander Newfoundland and how they opened their arms to the passengers of dozens of stranded commercial jetliners, diverted to Canada because of 9/11.

I have seen this show twice before in London and wish every Canadian and every American could find the time and opportunity to see it. It restores one's faith in humankind. Without my meaning to sound judgemental, this two hour show demonstrates as much about what it means to be a Christian as going to church every week likely does; charity, consideration, compassion, kindness, respect, grace and fellowship. For good measure a healthy dose of humour and some sorrow is also included. If you want to measure your contribution in the world, just see this play.

In case it isn't clear, I love London. I was born and spent my first twenty years in a city called New Westminster, nicknamed the Royal City, after Westminster in London. Both my parents grew-up in New Westminster as well, they during the halcyon years of the 50's and 60's. New Westminster was a wonderful place to grow up for me and for them as well based on the stories they tell. I am certain most former and current residence will attest to this being a special place. It is likely that my place of birth was the genesis of my being such an avid anglophile. Even to this day the 'Royal City' stills hold a traditional English May Day celebration complete with youngsters dancing the maypole. No Morris Dancers, however!

The late Queen, Elizabeth II, visited the City several times over the years and apparently, according to my Mom and Dad anyway, I got to wave to her when I was barely 1 year old. She and Philip were visiting on the Royal Yacht Britannica. The Britannica was moored right downtown after sailing up the Fraser River to the heart of 'the Royal City.'

After buying my theatre ticket for this evening's show I spend the rest of the day revisiting some favorite old haunts including the Churchill War Rooms, the City of London Museum, and the Tate Modern. I walk to all of these places as well.

Lunch is at a small pub near St. Paul's Cathedral where Christopher Wren was rumored to have stayed when rebuilding the Cathedral after the Great Fire of London. It is hard to beat a nice ale pie and a pint of bitter for lunch in such an historic setting.

Another reason I love London so much. These historic properties, both big and small, are everywhere. When in London, or any famous city, just go for a walk and follow your nose. You will be amazed at what you might see or discover.

I walk all the way back to the hotel. It is over three miles. Did I tell you I love to walk and have been on a least one week-long European hiking trip every year for the last decade or more? I have walked all over the U.K., including the entire West Highland Way in Scotland and the full length of Hadrian's Wall. But I have also hiked in France, Italy, Croatia, Slovenia, Malta, Spain (the Camino de Santiago de Campostela), and numerous other countries on the European Continent. Hiking is a great way to see a country up close and, again, to meet some very fine people.

I am back at the hotel by four o'clock and pleased to find that no one else has tried to get into my room. After a bit of a lie down, a shower, and a change of clothes I grab the tube back to Tottenham Court tube station for an early (by London standards anyway) dinner before the 'Come from Away' show.

The restaurant I want to dine at is on Charing Cross, as is the theatre I have tickets for. Both are very close to the book store I visited first yesterday.

While walking down Charing Cross toward the book store I am surprised to see the book store entrance has been blocked by police tape. There are several looky loos loitering in front and, being more than just a bit curious, I ask one of them if they know what is going on. An older gentleman, nattily dressed in sports jacket and school tie, answers me:

"I own Heritage Books the store half a block down," he says. "I noticed the closed sign on the door almost all day yesterday and most of today. The store never closes during the day, or at least very rarely. Knowing my old friend, Milton, the owner, has been quite ill I got curious and wandered over. I knocked and when no one answered I tried the door. It was open despite the Closed Sign.

When I went in I found the young fellow that works for Milton lying on the floor. He had been badly beaten and scarcely breathing. Before I called 999, I tried to talk to him asking if he was alright. He was obviously in great pain but kept mumbling something about papers, about Abraham Lincoln, and about two big men. He was making no sense. I called the police and emergency services right away and that is about all I can tell you. They just took him away by ambulance. Johnny, the young fellas name is Johnny."

After the shock of hearing about the beating the store clerk took, and being able to put two and two together, it is apparent that Clean and his little mini-me friend, Jerk, are after me and the document. How do I keep it safe and, even more importantly, how do I keep myself safe?

I decide it is wise to skip the show, a big personal disappointment. I opt instead, to go to the most crowded pub I can find in the Theatre District. There are lots of busy spots to choose from at this time of night given the after work crowds and the before theatre crowds are filling the streets, the pubs, and the restaurants.

I spy an unfamiliar pub, head directly over, and manage to find a spare table with only one chair left free. I have a light supper there without paying much attention to what I eat or to my pint. I am lost in thought. Doggedly determined, I decide to stay with my original plan to head north in the morning. Perhaps naively I feel I will be safe in Alnmouth. I will still be able to go to the Alnwick book store for document assessment. After that is taken care of, and if authentic, I can courier it safely to Andy or, if he can convince me to trust the Senator, then directly to the Senator. Once up north I might even be able to use the golf clubs I had sent directly to the U.K. after remortgaging the house to pay for their safe transport.

Following a rather unforgettable supper I take a taxi back to my hotel. Harder for my two would be shadows to follow me by taxi.

Safely back in my room I immediately call Andy. Again, fortunately, he is at his desk and not in class. I quickly update him on what has been going on over here, including a description of 'Clean and Jerk' and what they seem to have been up to.

"Andy, these two seem to be everywhere I go almost like they are ahead of me. I have no idea how they have been able to keep track. I guess I may have been too forthcoming about my plans. I think I mentioned Alnmouth in both book stores I went to yesterday so these two could well be heading up there next. They have obviously been questioning, and in one case maybe even brutalizing, people I have been in contact with. And I am pretty sure it was them that searched my Hotel room."

"What next Jay," Andy asks worriedly, "Are you thinking of coming home?"

"No, Andy,' I answer emphatically," I am not coming home. I am still off to Alnmouth in the morning but I have altered my plan slightly. I changed my train tickets and I did it on line so I couldn't be followed to the ticket office. My guess is these two will be onto me tomorrow when I board the train. Not many Flying Scotsman trains stop at Alnmouth on their way north to Edinburgh. So I have arranged to take the train only as far as York tomorrow. I will get off there and then catch a later train from York to Alnmouth. I think this should ensure I lose them."

I add, "Any word on this Ian Ralston character, Andy?"

"Nothing to report there yet. Everything about him seems to check out. No red flags. As for Senator Murchison, maybe we should let the Senator in on this a bit more. I thoroughly trust him, Jay. Maybe we should get a copy of the document to him for his advice. He has important contacts that may be able to help expedite or safeguard this, and, more importantly he can make sure you are safe."

"Worth thinking about, Andy, but let's leave it as is for now. I have a tentative plan and let's see how it works out once I get to Alnmouth. Talk later."

"Okay, Jay. Let me know if you change your mind. If you do, and I really think you should, I will facilitate a contact with the Senator for you. Stay safe and talk later."

Day 7

After a slightly better night's sleep, and my free small 'Full English Breakfast,' I take a morning train to York. It is only two hours from King's Cross up to York. As I just have an hour and a bit in York before the train to Alnmouth I just hang out at the Station. I am tempted to stay longer as, next to London, York is my favorite English city. Great place to visit, to walk the City walls, to explore the history of the Roman and Viking heritages, and learn about Richard the III.... "A horse, a horse, my kingdom for a horse."

York has one of the best railroad museums in the entire world. It includes complete Royal trains. The York Minster is my favorite church anywhere I have been in Europe, including the likes of Saint Peter's, Sacre Coeur, Saint Mark's Basilica, La Sagrada Familia and Notre Dame. Do I dare call the York Minster a church? What is the difference between a church, a Minster and a cathedral anyway? I should look that up one day.

Sticking with my plan, I catch the next northbound Edinburgh train out of York that stops at Alnmouth. This leg of the journey only takes about an hour and a half.

Nothing unusual or untoward happens on the trip up from York. As the station at Alnmouth is very small I had pre-booked a taxi into Alnwick so I could visit the book store and see their document expert straight away. An appointment with him had also been prearranged, another good reason for not staying longer in York.

A small owner-operator taxi is waiting for me at the Alnmouth station so I arrive in Alnwick and the bookstore in about ten minutes. On the way the taxi driver enthusiastically fills me in on the status of a potential locally run spur line from Alnmouth to Alnwick, the weather over the last few weeks, and the tenuousness of the current Prime Minister's hold on power in the U.K. You have got to love talking with the locals in these small towns and villages, especially taxi drivers. Who else knows more about local and world events?

Once driven comfortably and conveniently to the book store, I thank my new friend and I amble into this rather impressive and iconic facility. After a brief enquiry of the first staff person I see, I am directed to a small office on the upper floor. There I find the expert I am to meet with. However, before heading up, I left my suitcase at the front desk. The book store employees are, as always, accommodating and I didn't need to lug my case up the stairs with me.

The expert and I (the expert's name is Thomas Rhodes, by the way) meet in a small private office on the top floor of the book store. As I have already hinted at, this is not just any book store but one of the truly great ones anywhere, both for its ambience and, more importantly, for the quality of products, services, and expertise available.

After the polite niceties are dispensed with, I show Thomas Rhodes the Lincoln document. He is more than just interested. I would say he is thoroughly captivated.

His preliminary inspection suggests he believes it is authentic, but he tells me he needs at least two days to check aging patterns on the paper and to investigate the likelihood that the signature is also authentic. He thoughtfully expresses his view of just how significant and disruptive this document could prove to be if authentic. Together we both speculate on that for a while.

We then agree to meet face to face at 10.00 in the morning three days from now. Further we agree that confidentiality and safety are paramount and he assures me that this will be the case. In fact he gives me his solemn word and I believe him.

Business conducted, I take a brief stroll down the four or five blocks to Alnwick Castle and have a quick look around the castle and gardens. There is a small entry charge for the Castle but worth every penny or, should I say, worth every pence. It is always intriguing to me that this impressive castle, aka Harry Potter's Hogwarts School of Witchcraft and Wizardry, may have been in my own family, albeit it many, many hundreds of years ago.

Deeming my brief visit in town over, I retrieve my suitcase from the book store and find another locally operated taxi to take me into Alnmouth and the small cottage I have rented for the next ten days. Circumstances being what they are, whether I can stay for the full ten days in Alnmouth will depend on how things unfold. I supposed it all depends on what Thomas Rhodes finds and whether Sylvester and his little bald buddy, Tweety, show up. So much for the best laid plans etc.

The taxi driver drops me, and my suitcase, off at the rental cottage. After confirming that my golf clubs have been delivered intact, quickly unpacking, and familiarizing myself with my new accommodation, I wander through this small but delightful village in search of my favorite local pub and a pint. I see no evidence of the 'Bruise Brothers' and feel as relaxed as I have in the last week or so. Maybe I can even play some golf tomorrow!

I better check the bus schedule; remember I don't drive when in the U.K. So, once comfortably seated at the pub, pint in hand, I do a quick search of the internet for the bus service schedules. Happy with the bus times I can commute up the coast with, I then book a tee time at Dunstanburgh Castle Golf Course for ten the next morning. The pro shop tells me that, as a single player, they can easily fit me in if I am willing to join up with a threesome of club members. I eagerly agree. This is precisely what I want.

6

It is widely known that Senator Layton Conrad, the Senior Senator from South Carolina, will call a press conference any time he thinks he can garner a headline. Being one of the longest serving Senators in the U.S. Senate, six terms and counting, he will always attract an audience any time he calls a press conference. Point of fact, he has scheduled a press conference for today at 1.00pm. He has not specified exactly what he wants to announce but this, in itself, is not unusual for Senator Conrad.

Before approaching the dais to begin his announcement he has a private word with Mike Penn, a reporter from America First Press. He and Mike have had a long and mutually beneficial relationship. Quid pro quo, shared inside info, nudge, nudge, wink, wink etc. As a Senator it is always advantageous to have a few press people in one's pocket and he owns Mike 'The Penn is Mightier than the Sword' Penn outright.

His brief conversation with Penn goes like this, "Mike, after my opening statement I will open it up for questions as is normal. Wait for three of four questions to be posed and then ask to be called on. Once I call on you, ask me this question. I have written it down for you. Try and ask it naturally but earnestly. Don't screw it up. This is important."

The note he hands to the reporter reads as follows:

"Senator, rumours abound that, before he was assassinated, Abraham Lincoln issued some type of formal order stipulating substantial reparations be given to those who were enslaved prior to and during the hostilities of the American Civil War. Have you heard this rumour? If you have, do you have any comments about such an order, its potential validity, and its astronomical financial and land transfer ramifications today?"

The press conference then ensues and after an opening statement about the state of the economy, about how the current President is out of touch with the average American, and about how illegal immigrants are ruining the country, the Senator opens it up for questions.

After a half-dozen of the predicable questions about the performance of the sitting President, the economy, and legal and illegal immigration, Mike Penn is called upon.

"Yes, Mike, you have a question?"

"Senator, rumours abound that, before he was assassinated, Abraham Lincoln issued some type of formal order stipulating substantial reparations be given to those who were enslaved prior to and during the hostilities of the American Civil War. Have you heard this rumour? If you have, do you have any comments about such an order, its potential validity, and its likely astronomical financial and land transfer ramifications today?"

There is dead silence in the room and a lot of bewildered looks amongst the press gathered there and even amongst the Senator's staff. It is obvious no one else in the room had heard this rumour before, or if they have, not for many, many years.

"Well, Mike, yes, I have heard that rumour as well. While I cannot confirm the source it seems to be gathering momentum. I suspect it is another red herring initiated by those incompetents in power in Washington and likely planted by my esteemed colleague from California, Senator Murchison.

"Perhaps Senator Murchison has just awakened, or rather Woke, from one of those day dreams he spends so much of his time engaged in. Now he is trying to put his words into the mouth of one of the greatest Americans who ever lived, President Lincoln. It is time he, and those in his Party, focus their attention on matters at hand, not engaging in revisiting something that is over 150 years old and, quite frankly, is of no interest to the vast majority of Americans.

"Come on Senator Murchison", he adds, "Let's get with the program please and let's deal with issues that matter to today's American citizens. Not digging up dirt on the past nor spending billions on issues long since decided. Lincoln has returned from the grave? Really, Senator? What next? D-Day and the Apollo 11 moon landing were both staged? George Washington lied like a sidewalk? JFK is alive and living in Boca Raton? Teddy Roosevelt rode back down San Juan Hill in full retreat? Nonsense! It's all nonsense. Shame, shame, Senator Murchison, Shame on you!"

With that statement made the Senator calls an abrupt end to the conference and retreats stage right, pretending to be in a huff. The room is left abuzz.

Murchison and Conrad are both considered front runners for nominations from their respective parties for the next Presidential election to be held just over one year hence. There is no love lost between them. This salvo from Conrad will certainly not soften their animosities, personally or policy-wise.

Conrad has obviously succeeded in putting a negative spin on the issue as a precaution should the document currently being authenticated in England become publicly available. The battle for future public support has begun.

Day Eight

It does not take long for this rumour and the issue of reparations to receive national and even international attention. When Conrad speaks people listen. They don't always believe him, but they do listen.

Virtually all the national and regional newspapers, the major television networks, and the on-line media streams have picked up on it.

Headlines included the likes of:

- Conrad's fiery start to the Presidential debates begins early.
- What is Murchison Holding Back from us? The truth about the Lincoln Promise!
- Murchison accuses Conrad of out-and-out lying!
- Did Lincoln really promise to compensate slaves?
- Is this the document to end all documents? If yes, when do we get to see it?
- America's History—the Big, the Bad, and the Ugly... the restitution debate rekindled.

One of the most powerful and emotionally charged reactions came from Emanuel Sayer head of the Southern Baptist Coalition. When asked by a national network to comment he offered:

"Listen, I don't know what Senator Murchison knows or is hiding, if anything. I don't know what Senator Conrad knows or might be hiding, if anything. What I do know is for over 150 years black people in American have been waiting for an apology for being ripped out of their houses and beds, thrown onto ships, dragged half way around the world, and forced to do the white man's bidding. This went on not for weeks or months or years, not even for decades, but actually for centuries. Hell, the first slave arrived in Jamestown in 1619. Lincoln may be seen as the great liberator but it took 250 years for him, or someone like him, to step forward and actually liberate. Without giving him too much credit, we waited another 100 years for our voting rights to be properly recognized.

If you know the truth about America, much of its real wealth came from the South where cotton was king and America controlled the world supply and demand. It was the South that built this country's wealth not the North. If it wasn't for my ancestors and folks like them, slaving in fields for nothing but the privileges of being kept caged and underfed, this country may never have prospered. America the great may have just become another also ran nation in the Americas.

We, our black ancestors, built America and we deserve our fair share of its glory and of its wealth. Whether this, quote unquote, rumoured document exists or not ancestors of the slaves that built this Nation deserve an apology and they deserve it now. They deserve compensation, and in today's dollars and they deserve it now. They deserve credit for making America's wealth what is and they deserve that credit now. The voices of millions of black men, women and children are demanding justice and they deserve it NOW."

In rather hurried fashion the political pundit talk shows ramped up into high gear. Last night's late night TV was, as expected, full of political humor, silly rumours about dead Presidents, pretend political fisticuffs and funny assumptions and exaggerations. Some of the better one-liners from the late night monologues include:

- After Lincoln freed the slaves he apparently went to Dublin and chased all the snakes out of Ireland.
- They say Lincoln was a magician the way he steered the country through a civil war. Some speculate when he took off his stove pipe hat out popped 3 doves, a rabbit, a fake flower bouquet, and a magic wand.
- Did you hear that Washington had to cross back over the Delaware because he forgot to turn on his home security system?
- It is now alleged that George and Martha Washington were actually the same person...the first non-binary President. Now do you believe George couldn't tell a lie?
- Teddy Roosevelt charged up San Juan Hill not because he was brave but because he was being chased by a jealous husband.
- Lewis and Clark finally reached the West Coast today only to find McDonalds and Burger King had already set up 'trek through' windows.

Of all the hot topic news shows currently on TV, perhaps the most watched, and most influential, is 'America Tonight' on Trans Continental TV (TCTV). Tonight's show features, in large part, the topic of the rumours referred to in Senator Conrad's news conference. Given the controversy stirred up by Senator Layton Conrad, the show will garner a very large audience, even larger than usual.

Senator Murchison was invited to appear on the program but declined. He opted instead to send his new Communications Director, Ian Ralston.

Senator Conrad never puts himself in a situation he is not certain he can control, so he too declined the invitation. Instead, he is sending his would be Campaign Manager, Bartholomew Kendricks

An hour before the show is to air live Murchison phones Ralston and briefs him on the strategy he wants Ralston to employ in response to any questions posed by the moderator or the other panel members.

"Ian, it's me, Senator Murchison. I just wanted to brief you on what I expect from you, actually what I need from you, during the panel discussions on 'America Tonight.' Undoubtedly you will be asked to comment on the allegations made by that asshole, Conrad, on this so called Lincoln promise. In no uncertain terms are you to give any indication that we know anything about this rumour. And, of course, this is the truth. This needs to be made very clear.

"If asked, reply that you were as surprised by the allegations as Conrad purported he was surprised. I want you to emphasize that this appears to be nothing more than a stunt by Conrad to gain publicity and to skirt around the issue of reparations by turning it into some type of secret back room plan being hatched by our Party.

"When given the chance I want you to directly ask Conrad's political hack, Bartholomew Kendricks, if Conrad's press conference, and all the crap he was peddling there, was at the request of his friends the Brothers of Freedom."

"That might be a bit dangerous, Senator. We have no evidence that Senator Conrad has any affiliation or sympathy with the Brothers of Freedom. This could open the door for claims of slander."

"Slander, schmander, Ian. This is the chance for us to put him and his campaign on the defensive, which is exactly what he tried to do to us yesterday. Lay into that bastard Kendricks and make him sweat. Planting a hint about Brothers of Freedom is a must.

We need to help the public draw a clear and difficult to refute connection between white supremacists and Conrad. That is an important part of our election strategy. Clear?"

"Yes, Senator, I will see what I can do."

"Do more than just see what you can do Ian. Do it! I look forward to watching Kendricks, and by extension Conrad, squirm on live TV. We need to control the focus of the on-going political debate. I am depending on you to turn this thing back onto Conrad. This is our chance to squash that SOB. Let's make it count."

Moderator Todd Jennings opens the 'America Tonight' program with panel introductions:

"Good evening and welcome to another edition of 'America Tonight.' Joining us on tonight's panel are:

- from the *Washington Star*, feature columnist Myron Brownlow
- from the *New York Banner*, political columnist Janice Copeland
- from the White House, White House Press Secretary Sandra Pearson
- from Senator Conrad's campaign team, Campaign Manager Bartholomew Kendricks
- and from Senator Murchison's office, Director of Communications Ian Ralston.

"Later we will connect by video conference and hear from the renowned Professor of American History at Stanford University, and a noted Lincoln expert, Professor Andrew Hutchins.

"Panel, at his press conference yesterday, Senator Conrad raised an issue about a possible promise by President Lincoln, all those many years ago, that enslaved Americans deserved and hence are entitled to some type of reparations. This is an issue that both Senator Conrad and Senate Majority Leader Wilson Franks have long been openly against. Senator Murchison, by contrast, has long lobbied for a public apology from the government and for consideration of some type of reparations. While not omnipresent this has certainly become a real hot button issue of late. Myron, let's start with you. What is your take on this?

"Todd, I think this is a bit of a tempest in a tea pot. As far as I am aware this so-called rumour about a Lincoln promise was non-existent until Senator Conrad mentioned it yesterday. I think it is actually a figure of his imagination, not Murchison's. If not a figure of his imagination then it is a purposeful red herring designed to put Murchison and his campaign on the defensive."

Bartholomew Kendricks, Conrad's Campaign Manager, leaps in, "Come on Myron, you cannot be that naïve. Of course Murchison started this rumour and on purpose as well. It is part of his strategy. It is well known that he is in favour of some type of apology and restitution to ancestors of those enslaved in the South. Where there is smoke there's fire. He wants this to be a campaign issue and is dangling this out there as a way to ensure he has the Liberal vote and the Black vote, and in record turnout numbers, should he get the Party nomination. He is pandering to peoples' sense of guilt about the past. He could care less about any cost as long as he gets his name in lights."

A clearly agitated Sandra Pearson, White House Press Secretary, comes out in full attach mode. "Now who is being naïve Bartholomew? It is interesting that no one in the entire country, evidently except Senator Conrad, had ever heard this rumour and all of a sudden Murchison is supposed to have started it. Give me one example of where Senator Murchison referred to this so called Lincoln promise at any time in the past. Miraculously it emerges in the middle of a press conference initiated, diabolically it would seem, by his main political rival, Senator Conrad. Conrad is, and always has been, of the extreme right wing of his party and he will stop at nothing to gain whatever leverage he can with his ultra-conservative base, dirty tricks and all."

Kendricks jumps right back in. "Dirty tricks! Sandra, your party and your President elevated dirty tricks to an art form. It is the best news this Country has heard in years that the sitting President cannot run again. We have an opportunity to clean up the mess his seven years in office so far have left this country in. And Conrad is likely the best person, if not indeed the only person, capable of cleaning up this President's mess."

"Am I sensing sour grapes, Bartholomew? You and your Party are just jealous that you couldn't muster even close to enough votes to defeat the President in two consecutive elections, and it appears certain there will be a third straight loss by your Party next fall."

"Okay, okay, we all know partisan politics when we hear it," Todd Jennings interjects with a smile, "We have yet to hear from Ian or from Janice. First, to you, Janice, what is your take on this?"

"Well, Todd, you know what they say? Where there's smoke there's fire. At this juncture however I am not sure whose smoke it is and whose fire it is. Conrad is a pretty cagey politician and I think he may have just planted a big stink bomb on purpose."

Kendricks again dives back in, "Stink bomb! Stink bomb! The only bombs around here, Janice, are the duds you drop weekly in New York and call it a political column. It is time you stopped getting your advice from a medium, used some qualified researchers, and reported the facts, instead of the usual swill you deliver."

For perhaps the first times on live TV a single digit is held up by Janice Copeland and displayed prominently in the direction of Bartholomew Kendricks. Score one point for Janice!

Todd Jennings forcefully interjects with "Okay, okay, let us try and play nice, all of you. Ian Ralston, Ian, what is Senator Murchison's camp saying about all this?"

"The Senator is comfortable with his and his Party's position on current issues and we really have nothing to add to anything said regarding the rumours about Lincoln. Rumours are just that, rumours, no matter if they allude to Lincoln having made clear promises to ensure a great deal of land and vast amounts of money must be given as reparations."

"Ian, are you saying that Senator Murchison believes these rumours to be true?"

"I don't think I said that, Todd. I think I just said that our position, Senator Murchison's position, is a matter of public record and his beliefs about the entitlement of the ancestors of those enslaved is also a public record. He suggests such entitlements need to be met irrespective of the heavy costs to other Americans and regardless that over 150 years have passed in the interim."

"Well, Ian, I am not sure exactly what you are trying to convey here so I leave that up to our audience to interpret what Murchison wants. I think you might have been just a bit evasive.

"Before we leave this issue and move our talk to the recent economic numbers we have on the line, and on camera, from Stanford University, the esteemed History Professor, Andrew Hutchins. Professor Hutchins is a renowned expert on Abraham Lincoln, having published several books and journals on the life and times of the former President.

"Professor Hutchins, welcome."

"Thank you, Todd, and call me Andy. Professor Hutchins is a bit too formal. I encourage all my students to call me Andy as well. I should confess that my renown could be subject to considerable debate," he adds with a smile.

With a smile back, Todd Jennings continues, "Okay, Andy it is. Andy, I take it that you saw Senator Conrad's press conference yesterday and have been listening in to the dialogue here today. We would like your take on this whole idea that Lincoln may have actually initiated, or wanted to initiate, some type of formal policy of restitution."

"Happy to add my two-bits, Todd. I, of course, cannot speak for Lincoln. As I recall he was pretty good at speaking for himself. As for this rumour of a promise, in my research I often came across some suggestions that Lincoln had wanted to initiate some type of direct action on the reconciliation front before he was tragically assassinated. Lincoln was by no means unaware of the need to rebuild trust with the defeated South. He knew the country would not be able to move forward unless the North could reembrace the

South and invite people there to participate fully in a successful social and economic recovery and future.

"The economy of the South, one that relied so heavily of slave labour, was in a shambles. Properties were destroyed. Entire cities were destroyed. Heck we all can recall the scene from Gone with the Wind and the burning of Atlanta. That happened in real time back then.

"But Lincoln knew that it wasn't just white southerners he had to welcome back. All of a sudden there were nearly four million former slaves who also needed homes, jobs, and a sense of belonging to the newly reunited Union. How to rebuild the economy while welcoming back whites and blacks alike? No simple feat.

"I think Lincoln truly believed that a financially successful South depended on profitable and sustainable agriculture and, if slaves couldn't do the work for large landowners, the work would have to be done by small independent farms and farmers. This is essentially what helped build the success in the original Colonies and what makes much of the world work effectively to this day. I believe this is what he felt needed to be employed post war in the South.

"The outright granting of some small, personally owned, landholdings to former slaves, while ensuring that expert plantations owners still had enough property and potential to remain viable, would seem to be a wise strategy. If the former plantation owners, those with the agricultural expertise, couldn't use slaves but wanted to continue to successfully produce cotton or rice or beans or whatever then a workforce in need of employment, supported by a cadre of small, independent farmers, would also need to be readily available. And the potential for this two prong approach was certainly present.

"I honestly cannot comment on whether any formal document actually exists but, given what I believe Lincoln's mindset must have been in 1865, I cannot help but think that he would have at least tried to initiate some type of redistribution of lands and capital had he lived. How else could the South recover economically?

"So, in short, I would not be in the least bit surprised if Lincoln did issue a declaration of some sort. I am not sure that Secretary of State Seward and Lincoln were on the best of terms by War's end. Vice-President Andrew Johnson, actually a Democrat, apparently favored quick restoration of the seceded states to the Union without protection for the newly freed people who were formerly enslaved. So, with the sudden death of Lincoln, things may have taken a dramatic turn in an opposite direction to what Lincoln intended. Things could have mysteriously or miraculously, depending on your point of view, disappeared. Also remember, Lincoln was just beginning his second term.

"I cannot confirm the substance of the rumour that Senator Conrad alluded to nor, of course could I even begin to comment on who might have initiated it nor how. But I am not surprised, and would not be surprised, should it turn out to be true."

"Wow, thanks for that, Professor Hutchins, I mean Andy. Great insight and plenty of food for thought. I know the panelists are anxious to ask you some questions but our sponsors are even more anxious that we give them their due time. We also have to discuss what we think of the latest economic numbers. So we leave the issue of the Lincoln rumours for now, move directly to a commercial break, and when we return, we will discuss the recent economic numbers with our panelists."

No sooner had the program ended than Ian Ralston's phone rang. Not his newest burner phone but his official office phone. He picked it up on the second ring. It was Senator Murchison.

"Ian, what in God's name was that all about? I had asked you specifically to try and nail Kendricks' and Conrad's asses to the proverbial ground. You completely let them both off the hook. What you said was vague and even hinted at you being in Conrad's corner. I sure as hell hope that isn't true. What the hell did you think you were trying to do?"

"Senator, I hope I didn't bugger things up for you. It certainly wasn't my intention. You had to be there to get a sense of how to respond to the questions posed. I felt, at the time, that it was best for us to maintain a cool demeanour thereby showing our, rather your, campaign to be one of quiet reason and steadiness. We don't want to come across as flighty, angry and reckless. We need to be seen as Presidential not appear like petulant teenagers who are mad because we are not getting our own way."

"Ian, I can see what you were trying to do but I think we missed a wonderful opportunity to put those sons of bitches in a corner. Remember this is my campaign, not yours. I welcome and appreciate your advice but, in the future, if you want to go in a different direction than I have asked you to, please run your thoughts by me before you head off on your own. Understood?"

"Yes, Senator, understood."

Ralston had no sooner hung up from talking with Senator Murchison that his burner phone rang.

"Ian, it's Tyrone. Good job on the panel tonight. I don't think anyone listening in has any idea what the hell Murchison stands for."

"Thanks, Tyrone."

"I am pretty worried however about what that guy from Stanford said. Reading between the lines it seems this Lincoln document has a pretty good chance of being legit. We may need to increase the pressure on this Alexander guy. Whatever he is toting around England cannot ever see the light of day. I think I better give Gunnar and Wyatt a ring and see what is going on over there. Those two morons best get their shit together and clean this thing up once and for all. Talk later and keep a close watch on Murchison. If he even hiccups, I want to know about it."

"Good luck with Gunnar and Wyatt, Ralston replies, "And yes, I hear you about Murchison, I won't let him out of my sight. Talk later."

7

Day Nine

As it is early morning in the U.K., Tyrone has to wait until much later to call Gunnar and Wyatt. When the appropriate time to call finally arrives, and the call is made by Tyrone, Gunnar picks up his burner on the third ring.

"Gunnar, it is Tyrone. The shit seems to be edging very close to the fan back here. I know I suggested you two lie low for the next day or two after getting caught out lying about Alexander's hotel room and nearly putting the book store guy into the morgue. But I think we need to step up the pressure on this asshole. Are you both up in Alnmouth? Good! See if you can take a more direct approach with this guy. Put the squeeze on him. Senator Conrad wants that document to see the bottom side of a paper shredder. Get to it and keep me in the loop. And try not to kill anyone or beat anyone else half-to-death, that is unless you have to. And, for Gods-sake, buy a hat one of you. Parading around like you normally do you likely stand out like two mushrooms in a newly paved parking lot."

With that conversation over, Tyrone signs off and dials Senator Conrad immediately.

"Senator, it's me, Tyrone, and yes this call is safe. You certainly loosed the cat amongst the pigeons with that Press Conference. I bet Murchison is shitting his pants. Ian kept his mouth well shut too, didn't he? I loved the remark about 'no matter the cost.' And that history professor sure helped give credence to your accusations that the Senator may have been complicit in starting this rumour. Touché."

"Yes, Tyrone, job done and done well. So far Ian has proved to be a real asset, a real profitable plant in Murchison's garden. Enough of that though, what is happening in the U.K. with those two dopes you sent over?"

"Easy on them Senator. They have their uses. No luck so far but they have a bead on this guy and will catch up with him in the next day or two I am certain. I have given them some pretty clear instructions to do whatever it takes to get the job done and get it done they will. I know you don't think much of them but I have stood beside them in many difficult situations here and in the Middle East and they have always stepped up. They will always have our backs. We need to have theirs. Trust me and trust them."

"Okay, Tyrone, I am trusting you on this. We can't take much more bad news. I am trying to run for President and there are lots of people watching. Our base is solid as solid can be but that won't get us over the top next fall. And then to add to our list of calamities I just found out this morning that one of our most prominent supporters from Texas, that pious TV preacher we own, has been diddling more than just the hens in his flock. Turns out he has been diddling the chicks too. To make matters worse he has been flying all over the State of Texas in his private airplane, delivering the good word from the good book, while being accompanied by a 17-year-old co-ed he has been personally preaching to... if you get my gist."

"Jesus Christ, Senator. This couldn't get much worse. That stupid smug sanctimonious asshole."

"Couldn't get much worse! Couldn't get much worse! Ha! Let me tell you how worse it can be.

"Turns out he knocked her up and, to keep it quiet, arranged for an abortion last month. The stupid son-of-a-bitch has been front and centre in the pro-life campaign down there for decades and he has been flying my banner at every opportunity. Now that an abortion he allegedly paid for has become public knowledge every news outlet in the Country is going to make this the lead item tomorrow. We just grabbed the headlines with the Lincoln rumour and then lost them within a matter of hours.

"My people here are going to have to get on this right away and distance ourselves, as far as humanly possible, from that nit-wit of a preacher. As I said, our base is solid gold but that doesn't get us all the votes we need next fall. We can't afford too many major set-backs. Make sure your two in the U.K. don't do anything stupid, and tell them to get this done right and get it done right away. Shit, shit, shit!"

With that final sentiment expressed, the Senator hangs up leaving Tyrone to have to deal with his own anxieties and doubts.

8

Day Ten

I am now back at my delightful little rental cottage at the end of another very good day. I have enjoyed two successive days of relaxation, golfing on both days, and fitting in leisurely walks on the lovely Northumberland beaches.

The beaches here are great for long, unhurried, walks over pretty white sand, up and down enormous dunes while never needing to skirt too much litter or rubble. Pristine is the one word that comes to mind to describe them.

These shore walks are resplendent with every mix of dog imaginable along with a mix of sometimes harder to describe owners. Again my fancy lets loose as I invent stories about many of those out walking their dogs and about their dogs. It is always fun to compare how much dogs resemble their owners or how owners eventually morph into the spitting image of their dogs. Now I have to wonder, do I look like a Jack Russel Terrier? Sometimes I think I really need to grow up but why hurry when it is so much fun to be a kid?

The sun has been out since I arrived up north. It is unseasonably warm. Best of all there has been no sightings of Abbott and his little buddy Costello. It seems I have gotten some holiday time after all and squeezed in some great golf too.

I shot ninety-one yesterday on the course at Dunstanburgh Castle. I played off the yellow tees. The course plays just a bit less than 6000 yards off those tees and is a par 70. You get lots of roll on the dry fairways, which is good for ones ego. Not my best score by a mile but it would have been much better had the scenery not been so distracting. That is my excuse anyway. Golfers are allowed to make excuses. That is what makes the game bearable, if not great.

They have these wondrous sand dunes here to admire as you walk along the fairways. Further it is difficult to concentrate while hitting an approach shot into a green when a mere 100 yards behind that same green looms the ruins of a fourteenth-century castle. Where in the world can you play golf like this and by bus no less?

At Dunstanburgh I played with three locals who graciously treated me to a nice late lunch and a great pint or three afterwards. Longtime chums of each other, these three entertained me with hilarious stories about the area and about each other. The stories came out one after another after another. Each story funnier than the previous one.

My favorite story was told by Jake. Jake hails from the nearby village of Seahouses. As Jake tells it, "A woman got on a bus with her baby. The driver said, 'Ugh! That's the ugliest baby I've ever seen.' The woman stalked off to the rear of the bus and sat down. She turned to the man sitting next to her and said, 'The driver just insulted me!' The man said, 'You go and give him a telling off. I'll hold your monkey for you.'"

Jake then challenged me to contribute my own favourite. "You must have a lot of good stories about Canada. Come on, Jay, give it a go."

I responded by saying that, "I do have a lot of great stories about Canada but one of my favorite personal stories actually took place while I was working in China a few years ago."

I told them my longish story as follows:

"When trying to shop in the silk market in Beijing I found it difficult to buy anything. The market is a large complex, several stories high, with booth after booth of items for sale, from toys to clothes to sports equipment to electronics. I found it difficult to cope with the pressure brought on by the sales vendors, especially as I spoke no Chinese. Every stall I walked by had a sales person who would offer something or ask something, often quiet aggressively. So I just awkwardly wandered on without feeling comfortable enough to buy anything. It was frustrating as I knew I needed to bring some gifts home with me.

"When I had the chance, I asked a Chinese colleague I was working with how to shop successfully in the silk market. She laughed, but then graciously taught me three phrases in Chinese. She said all that I needed was to be able to say these three things in Chinese:

- 'I am just looking.'
- 'How much is it?'
- 'That's too much.'

"She then told me that, when I walk around the silk market, and anyone pressures me, just say (in Chinese obviously) 'I'm just looking.' The vendor(s) will then leave you alone to wander.

"She then added that, if I wanted to buy something at a specific vendor, once they spoke to me, just respond in Chinese with 'How much is it?' She went on, no matter what the vendor answers (you won't understand it anyway, she said, laughing), just reply with (again in Chinese), 'That's too much.'

"She continued, Once you say 'that's too much', invariably the sales vendor will then hand you a calculator displaying the price they want for the item. You then enter a counter offer on the same calculator. I recommend starting at 10% of the vendor's price or else you will get fleeced. The vendor will enter a new offer and negotiation can proceed, back and forth, from there.

"Her advice worked like a charm. When I indicated, in my poorly pronounced 'I'm just looking' the vendors left me alone. I even got some nice smiles from the vendors for my attempts at speaking Chinese.

"When asking, 'How much is it,' I found this worked equally well. I made several purchases and was so proud of myself. Again, several vendors seemed delighted and respectful of my efforts to speak in Chinese. They were obviously humoured by my less than perfect Chinese pronunciation but they seemed to appreciate the attempt.

"All was well until I got quite obviously and quite aggressively propositioned by a young Chinese woman. In her halting English she said to me, 'Do you like my thighs?' and proceeded to rub up against me."

I concluded my longish story by telling my three new friends, "You cannot imagine how difficult it is to fend off the advances of a determined lady of the evening when all you can say in her language is 'How much is it', that's too much' and 'I'm just looking.'"

My three new buddies roared with laughter.

All said and done, it was a lovely afternoon, especially with these three. This is exactly why I come here year after year. Great golf but, even more importantly, great people.

This morning I followed yesterday's game with an eighty-three at the Warkworth Golf Course, barely ten minutes by bus south of Alnmouth. See why I love the buses over here?

Eighty-three is several strokes better than my average score at home. This course at Warkworth is a par seventy-one. Again it plays about 6000 yards off the white tees. It was a little easier than yesterday as there was no fourteenth-century castle in the fairway to distract me.

I again played with three locals and had another terrific time. Not as many belly laughs but plenty of good conversation and a lot of questions about life in Canada. I was surprised by their asking me my opinions about what is happening stateside these days. It seems everyone is interested, if not outright worried, about the divisiveness that seems to be so omnipresent down in the U.S. I think people believe that a stable America makes for a stable world. I whole-heartedly concur.

The Warkworth Golf Course is another lovely links course and Warkworth village itself is another of those near-perfect

Northumberland villages. The village boasts some of the finest pubs anywhere. I can certainly attest to the two pubs my golf companions and I visited. I also took the time to take a peek into a perfect little twelfth-century church. I would have had a better look around but it is difficult to wander among church pews when you have fourteen golf clubs strapped to your shoulder.

Somewhere in my past genealogical research I learned that Warkworth Castle, the centre piece of this pristine village, may have been in our family a mere 800 years or so ago. Maybe I should claim ownership of the Castle and surrounding lands. Why not? If Lincoln's influence can reach forward 150 plus years, why can't I reach back 800? One can dream, can't one?

Still no sign of the Bruise Brothers. If they are up here somewhere I guess they haven't been checking the bus stops as that has been my mode of golf transportation. Someone on the bus today asked me, with a wink, if I had any whisky in my golf bag. I said no but I do have a nice set of china and some silverware if you want to join me for dinner. Everyone within ear shot laughed. I am a regular card!

I am back at the cottage with visions of even par rounds of golf floating in my head. Now that is really imagining things. The cottage I have rented has an old PVR and I had it set to record for last night's airing of 'America Tonight.' I usually try and tune in whether at home or abroad.

No matter where I go in the world I always try and keep up with current events. You don't often get much news from Canada when travelling abroad but you can always get news from one of those 24 hour news channels about what is happening south of the border. Keeping abreast of what is going on down there is very important. Former Prime Minister Pierre Trudeau once said to his U.S counterpart, President Nixon, "Living next to you is in some ways like sleeping with an elephant. No matter how friendly and even-tempered is the beast, if I can call it that, one is affected by every twitch and grunt."

So, hopefully without sounding rude, it is always important to see what or who is twitching and grunting below the 49th parallel.

As I watch the recording of 'America Tonight' on the PVR I am thunder-struck by the conversation about Lincoln and the references to some type of Lincoln promise. I am also taken aback by seeing first, Ian Ralston, and next seeing one of my closest friends, Andy Hutchins, live on TV. I am not quite sure what to make of what I see and hear.

Who let the cat out of the bag? Senator Murchison? That Ralston guy? Hopefully not my good pal, Andy?

Ralston makes me nervous as he really didn't do much to help Murchison's cause. His statement about "no matter the cost' could be taken a number of ways and most of those ways are not supportive of his boss's stated position. And then Andy went on and on about the possibilities of some type of promise of restitution, or at least he believed that Lincoln intended to move in that direction given time. Lincoln was only into the fourth month of his second term when he was assassinated so who knows what he might have done with more time. So, Andy's assessment has to be considered fair. Of course he also has seen the copy of the alleged Executive Order to help inform him.

It is obvious I need to get this authentication work done and get this damn document into someone else's hands or into a paper shredder ASAP. Fortunately I am supposed to get the verdict tomorrow from Thomas Rhodes at the Alnwick bookstore. I certainly intend to keep that meeting and I, for sure, best call Andy later tonight to find out what in the hell is going on.

It is now seven o'clock in the evening. Having watched the recorded American Tonight and taken some time to reflect on its content, it is time to saunter out for some supper. I quickly shower and change out of my golf duds. I put on some chinos and the new golf shirt I bought at the course today. I have a life philosophy that a person can perhaps have too much success in life, and even too much money in the bank, but they can never have too many golf shirts.

There are three lovely small pubs in Alnmouth but I have my favorite and I am off to it for a cottage pie and a pint of bitter. I know a few of the staff so it is always like old home week for me. The pub only seats about twenty-five people max so it is a smallish 'old home'. The pub also doubles as an Inn, letting a few rooms per night. That allows the Inn to flourish even with such a small capacity for pub patrons.

When I get to the pub, there are only two other patrons in the place. They are being served by a youngish bartender whom I have not met before. No 'old home week' staff on duty tonight.

The other two patrons are an elderly couple, each several years older than me; at least I assume they are. My ego talking? Maybe I need a good look in a mirror to see how old I am.

By way of comparison, the bartender is so young that he barely needs to shave.

All three are listening to a 70s' soundtrack that is playing, and debating their favorite 70s' songs. Despite being born about five decades later than the couple, the bartender is enthusiastically engaging in the debate. Young people today seem to be gravitating to some of the classic rock music of the past. If one is to listen to today's popular electronic music it should hardly come as a surprise they want to look backward for inspiration and quality. 'Get off my lawn.'

I was born in 1970, so one would think I was also too young for this era. Actually, according to music aficionados, there were really several different music eras of 70s' music. Because both my parents loved this music there was always something from the 60s' or 70s' playing at our house when I was a youngster. I was raised with their stories of famous local music venues like New Westminster's Denny's Discotheque, Magilla's and the Grooveyard and Vancouver's iconic Oil Can Harry's. So, I too grew to love this music, all of it, with perhaps a minor preference for classic soft rock; Dan Fogelberg, Jackson Browne, James Taylor, the incomparable Jimmy Buffett, and the like. But, hell I even like Disco.

I am enjoying the conversation with the three of them and enjoying the pint and enjoying my life at this juncture.

The topic has recently moved to what is the greatest movie soundtrack of all time. I have just mentioned American Graffiti, The Commitments and The Big Chill as my votes, when the door opens and in walks the two Bruise Brothers. They spot me immediately and head straight for my table.

My Dad always used to say, "Sit with your back to the wall in a strange bar, Jay, as you never know who might walk in." I have always followed his advice and I always will. Because of that, these two take seats opposite me and essentially have me trapped against the wall.

This is the first time I have had a look at Mickey and Goofy up close. The taller one is about six two and built. The guy looks like he could crush cars with his eyebrows. He has a clean shaven head and, like my friend at the London hotel, Rosa, suggested, he has a swastika tattoo prominently displayed on his neck. He has the typical skull-shaped oversized ring on one hand and tattoos of seemingly random letters on his knuckles. He is dressed in black pants and black tee, but sports a brown bomber jacket with some kind of prominent patch from Idaho on it.

His mini-me partner is only about five six but just as solidly built. No swastika that I can see but lots of other ink. He has on a white tee and is sporting black jeans, a light camo jacket, and a camo ball cap to match. The hat doesn't quite cover up the fact that he too has a shaved head. Oddly, the hat still has the price tag hanging off one side. I suspect he doesn't know that, but maybe it is a new fashion trend.

The bigger of the two says to me, "Small world, Mr. Alexander. We have been looking for you and this might be as good a place as any to have a chat."

"Well, well," I reply, "If it isn't Archie and Jughead. Are you two having fun running around England beating up book shop clerks?"

I have never been particularly good at fisticuffs but when it comes to insults and sarcasm I can more than hold my own. I offer a big thank you to my three older sisters for teaching me to think on my feet and fight back, albeit only verbally.

"Who the fuck are Archie and Jughead?" the bigger guy says, challenging me with a fixed stare. Then he adds, "You have something we want and I suggest we hop in our car outside, head up to that quaint little cottage you are ensconced in and pick it up. Once we have it you can get back to your nice little life and we can be on our merry way."

"Ensconced? Quaint? Pretty fancy words for a bullet-headed gorilla like you," I counter. "Have you been reading one of those 'learn a new word a day books' while shaving your bald head each morning? I am not going anywhere. I have already ordered a nice cottage pie and am going to sit here and enjoy it and enjoy my pint. So, just fuck off and leave me alone."

Actually I have not ordered any dinner yet but they don't need to know that. Plus I am not really as calm and self-confident as I pretend to be. I am trying to bide my time until I can think of a way out of this mess. I don't think the older couple or the twelve year old bartender would be much help.

The mini-me guy pipes in, "Once we drag your ass outside, and are finished with you, even ice cream will be a tough swallow. Now, get your skinny butt out of the chair and let's go outside right fucking now." As he says that, he puts a steel grip on my left arm.

Just as things are about to get nasty for me, the pub door opens and three people walk in, a man and two women. As soon as I see who it is I feel an enormous sense of relief. I know all three of these people, and my escape from Dumb and Dumber may be at hand.

Of the three newcomers, the man looks at me and breaks out laughing. "Why it's Jay Eh," he announces with an ear-to-ear grin.

Quite an unusually wide ear-to-ear grin too thanks to his athletic past, and his two very distinctive cauliflower ears.

The fellow bellowing at me is Ray Benjamin and he is a great friend. He is also a retired Inspector from the Northumbria Police. He stands about 6'6" and could still play a mean second row forward with the Alnwick starting fifteen in Rugby even if he is few years older than my fifty-three years. As a result of his Rugby playing days he is proudly displaying those two enormous cauliflower ears and a wide, clearly too often broken, nose.

Despite the sports scars he is still improbably handsome and is as fit as a fiddle. He could still kick the ass of any would be felon and my ass too I should add without too much surprise to anyone. In fact he has kicked my ass many times, fortunately for me just in golf.

Ray is a very distant relative of the famous Harry 'Hotspur' Percy known for his border wars with the Scots, his action during parts of 100 Years' War with the French, and his prominence is Shakespeare's play Henry IV. There is a very prominent statue of 'Hotspur' at the entrance to Alnwick Castle. Like Ray, most anyone born in this part of the world likely has Percy blood running through their veins

The Percys have never been anyone to trifle with and they have been the dominant family in Northumberland for over 700 years. The Percys still own and have a residence in Alnwick Castle today (likely stolen from my family, ha ha). It is said the Percy family still control 100,000 acres of land in the area. As for the famed courage and daring of Harry Hotspur and generations of Percy men, Ray is no exception.

Ray is sporting his usual plaid shirt, old guy jeans, a knock off gore-tex jacket, and hiking boots. He is not known as a fashion plate. He always teases me about my clothes, calling me Mr. Barbour and Mr. Burberry. I have known him for about eight or nine years. Em and I befriended Ray and his wife that long ago when we were staying in Alnmouth. In fact we met him and his wife in this same pub, often dining together and later teaming up for pub quiz nights.

He always calls me 'Jay Eh' instead of Jay A. because I am Canadian and because he thinks it is funny to add the Eh instead of the A... and actually it is funny, as is Ray, he is hilarious in fact.

When I think of his name, Ray Benjamin, I always think of an ex-boss who used to talk about a number of my staff whom he said had backward and forward names, names like Peter Morris (or Morris Peter), Gerard James (James Gerard) and Gardner Ross (or (Ross Gardner). In Ray's case it is Raymond Benjamin or Benjamin Raymond. Funnily, I should add on a personal note, there is also Jay Alexander or Alexander Jay.

I was planning on phoning Ray in the next day or two to set up a visit with him and his lovely wife or for a game of golf, but I wanted to get the document authentication out of the way so I could feel comfortable talking with them. Keeping a secret from Ray Benjamin is not an easy thing to do.

Of the two women with Ray, I know both, as I have said. One is his wife Maggie or as he calls her either Mags or Magpie. Mags is a terrific woman. High spirited, quick witted and loves to laugh. She is always up for an adventure. She can also be quite forthright when necessary and, as a result, she rules the roost at home and certainly Ray knows who the boss is.

Mags is wearing what she normally wears, the latest outdoor fashions from Cotswold and Arc'teryx. She has a shock of curly red hair, a touch too much makeup, and big dangly hoop earrings that look like owls. She is pretty in a very windswept, frenetic and intense way. She is a whirlwind of fun and vitality. Whenever she enters a room the mood elevates and the energy becomes almost palpable.

The other woman with Ray and Mags perhaps poses a bit more of a problem for me, actually more than just perhaps.

Her name is actually Darlene, but everyone calls her Darcy. She is Mags' younger sister and she and I have some history.

Apparently when growing up she, Darlene, was a real handful. The youngest of five children, she was incredibly adventurous, often argumentative and had (and I can attest still has) a temper.

Her full name is Darlene Cecelia McDougal. Given her propensity, as a child, to get into her mother's bad books, her mother was often heard yelling "Darlene Cecelia McDougal, stop that." Later, dropping the last name, it became easier to yell, "Darlene Cecelia, get down from there." Later still it was shortened further to, "Darlene Cecile, just do as you are told." Eventually it became more convenient for her mother and her older siblings to just shorten it to "Dar Ce, cut that out." Hence everyone called her Darcy and that is the name that her family eventually adopted for her and the name everyone knows her by today. If you were to poll 100 of her friends and colleagues I suspect only two or three of them would know her real name is Darlene.

About eighteen months ago, oddly also about the same length of time after Em had passed away, Ray and Mags introduced her to me in this same bar. She was visiting them from her home in Berwick-Upon-Tweed, about thirty-five miles north and on the border with Scotland. She is Mags' younger sister and also her best friend. She is easily as pretty as Mags, prettier actually, but in a more classic, less frenzied way.

Darcy and I hit it off almost the moment we met. She was just getting over a messy divorce and, even though it had been a year and a half for me, I was still suffering quite badly from losing Em. I think the time for each of us to move on with our lives had just reached a tipping point. We both seemed to have arrived at a place that made us willing to take a chance.

As quickly as we hit it off upon first meeting, we became more than friends almost faster. We began seeing each other and actually tried a long distance relationship for about ten months. We spent a fortune on the phone almost every night (day in my case, night in her case), there is an eight hour difference remember.

She came to visit me in Canada twice and I reciprocated. She met and liked my kids and I, in turn, got to know her children and liked them very much. She has a boy and girl just like Em and I did. We are both of the same vintage, albeit she is four years younger and, all would agree, she is much better looking than I am too.

Sadly our relationship broke down when she wanted a more permanent arrangement. I think I did too. Actually I know I did too. However neither of us was prepared to move 8000 miles to make this happen. She is a physiotherapist with a thriving practice in Berwick and did not want to leave her practice or her two children who both live near her in Berwick. There is also one grandchild, a five year old little girl named Maggie, named after her sister.

I am a Canadian, actually a British Columbian, through and through, and didn't want to leave my kids or my lovely seaside abode. It has been about eight months since we last spoke and, as I recall, her last words to me were "Fuck you, Jay."

The 70s' soundtrack has just started playing 'Fly like an Eagle' by Steve Miller and I take this as a good omen. I seize the opportunity to escape Popeye and Bluto and stand up and cross the floor to embrace these three, well at least embrace two of them anyway.

Bluto says to me as I stand up, "This isn't over asshole."

Popeye adds, "Nice cottage you rented by the way. Gunnar, let's get the fuck out of here."

Both of them get up and storm out of the pub. As I make my escape I think that maybe I need to change my pants.

As I cross the pub floor, Ray races over to greet me and gives me a big bear hug, near kills me. Mags gives me a big hug as well, just not quite as crushing, and a nice wet kiss on the cheek, leaving a red lipstick impression that would be hard to explain if I was still married.

Darcy gives me a brief nod and, through a slightly sardonic smile, says, "Nice to see you Jay, it has been a while. How have you been? You look good." I am not sure she really means any of this. I still recall the "Fuck you, Jay" all too vividly.

"You look good too, Darcy. And I am fine," I reply, "And you?"

"Fine, just fine," she answers through a thinly veiled grimace.

Ray and Mags are standing next to us grinning like the proverbial Cheshire Cats, each enjoying how awkward this greeting is. They both know our history and, I believe, they secretly want us to reconnect. I am certain they care about both of us.

Mags breaks the ice by saying, "Let's grab a seat, all 4 of us, there is a table over there." She then quickly canvasses us for a drinks order and heads for the bar, a pint of bitter for me, a G and T for her, a glass of sauvignon blanc for Darcy and a Coke for Ray. Ray only drinks either Coca Cola or water and very little water.

Ray says to me, "Who were you two handsome friends? They look like they just stepped off the bus after getting early release from His Majesty's Prison Northumberland. It looked a bit intense there for a minute and trust me I have seen intense in my time."

"I'll tell you all about it, or at least some of it, once we get a drink and have a bit of a catch up on life. It is a long story."

"What is a long story, your life or your talking with those two?" Ray replies with a twinkle in his eye. He then turns and yells something out to Mags at the bar, I think he yells, "And bring some crisps, but not prawn flavoured," while I, somewhat awkwardly, turn my attention to Darcy.

She looks spectacular by the way. Just as beautiful as she did the first time I saw her. Auburn hair neatly cut and presented, bright brown eyes, evidence of a summer tan, and a hint of freckles, still slim, trim and, of course fit. What physiotherapist isn't fit?

She is always stylishly dressed in comfortable but well-chosen clothes. Her clothing is usually more outdoor than Dior although I am sure she would kill in Dior too. Very little make-up as none is ever really required. Also not much jewelry, except for a small cameo around her neck which I recall quite clearly I gave her for Christmas just before we ended things. The cameo is an encouraging sign. Not only didn't she throw it away, she still wears it. She clearly likes something I gave her. Most importantly, I notice there is no ring on her left hand. Still single I hope, I think to myself, fingers crossed.

Ray hops up and ambles to the bar to help Mags carry the drinks leaving us, purposefully I am sure, to break the ice.

We go through almost the same words again. How are you, you look well, you too, fine, fine etc.

I finally blurt out, "It really is nice to see you Darce (pronounced like farce). It has been a while. We didn't leave things in perfect shape when we last spoke. I am sorry the way we left it."

She replies in a somewhat edgy voice, "Yes, I suppose 'Fuck you Jay' wasn't the perfect Hollywood ending but I was angry and frustrated and, if I recall, you were being a bit of a dickhead."

Ouch, that hurt. Me a dickhead? Never!

Trying to ease the tension I think we both are feeling by this surprise encounter, I offer, "Well, the past is the past. We should try and put that aside, at least for now, and both put on a good front for Ray's and Mags' benefit. Besides we did like each other once. Can't we still be friends?"

She sort of smiles at me and says, "Okay, friends!"

I reply with a warmish (heavy on the ish) smile, "Okay, friends it is!"

Though I sense we are both holding a lot back, with the ice slightly cracked, even if not yet entirely shattered, we get on with having a pleasant evening, all four of us.

The talk over the next hour or so covers the usual subjects; houses, kids, grandkids, work (in Mags' and Darcy's case anyway), travel, golf, dogs, Brexit, Brexit regret and, sadly, the war in Europe. We share lots of laughs, revisit many old stories, talk a bit about the future and Mags and Darce even shed a few tears.

Then Ray changes the subject rather dramatically and asks me what the conversation with those two behemoths was all about. I respond as best I can by sharing what I think is safe to share without endangering anyone else at the table and without letting the entire cat out of the bag regarding the document and its potential impact.

I tell them about receiving an unusual bequest from a quite distant relative. I explain the Maureen connection and how this bequest came to me. I go on and explain that the bequest contained a document that could have some historical significance in the United States and was, prior to now, publicly unknown. I never mentioned Lincoln however or what the historical significant was, or could still be.

I remark that its existence is seen as a threat to certain right of centre people in the States. I explain that, because of this perceived threat, Popeye and Bluto have been following me. I suggest that they (Popeye and Bluto) are more than likely prepared to resort to violence to get what they want. Finally I tell them that the document has yet to be authenticated, that I have left it with an expert in Alnwick for review and assessment, and that I am to meet with this expert tomorrow at 10.00am to get the results. I finish up by saying how nervous I am, actually scared, about the whole thing and hope that it will all be over in a day or two. I don't mention the part about nearly soiling my trousers.

I do add that they, Popeye and Bluto, "Know where I am staying in Alnmouth. They told me that just before they stomped out of the pub. I am not sure if they will try and tackle me at the cottage tonight but, at a minimum, I am sure they will be on my tail to tomorrow."

Mags and Ray both pipe in, almost simultaneously, "You will stay with us tonight."

"We have lots of room," Mags adds. "Too much room these days if you listen to Ray. He wants to downsize. Darcy is staying overnight and has Jackson's room (their son having long since moved out) but we have 2 other empty bedrooms. What do you say?"

What I say to myself is how do you spell AWKWARD? Darcy and I under the same roof after just seeing each other again for the first time in more than 8 months and after a bad ending back then besides!

Truthfully, given the circumstances, what else can I say except, "Sounds like a plan, at least until I can get things sorted out tomorrow. Are you sure no one minds," I say to Mags but really addressed to Darcy.

Mags and Ray both say simultaneously, "Great, it is decided then."

Darcy merely takes a great big breath and, while seeming to still be inhaling, says, "Well I guess we better get going back to your place then, Mags."

We all climb into Ray's English sized (aka pint sized) SUV and drive the few blocks down the road to their house. When I bought my SUV back home I told the sales person I needed room for five adults and a back space large enough to accommodate four sets of golf clubs.... road trips with the boys. In the U.K. you can barely fit four people and one set of golf clubs into an SUV and, then, only as long as all the doors and all windows are open. I am exaggerating of course. There I go insulting people again. Maybe I really am a dickhead.

We take a long and rather elaborate route to make sure we are not being followed. I think we pass three golf courses, a hospital, four primary schools, two seniors' complexes plus a cricket pitch before we arrive at Ray's house which, as the crow flies, is actually less than one kilometer from the pub.

We all get comfortable in Ray's and Mags' sitting room, a cup of coffee in front of three of us and Ray with another Coke. However I still need to check in with Andy, especially after seeing his and Ralston's performances on the taped recording of 'America Tonight.'

I ask permission from Mags to borrow their den to make a phone call, excuse myself, and go in and dial Andy's number on my cell. Fortunately he is not in class and picks up on the second ring. Sometimes I wonder if he has any classes at all!

"Andy, it's Jay. I am checking in to see what is up. Things are getting pretty hairy over here. I saw you on 'America Tonight.' Actually I saw you, Ralston and that Kendricks guy. It seems like that document I copied to you last week has taken on a life of its own. Interesting as the only people who have seen it are you and I. What the hell is going on, Andy?"

"I wish I knew, Jay. The rumours referenced in the press conference by Senator Conrad seemed to have come out of the blue. I spoke the truth when I talked about Lincoln on the program the other night. I know a lot about Lincoln and really believe he would have acted on the restitution front had he had time, unless of course he did act and it wasn't actioned for one reason or another, all of them sinister.

"Jay, rumours around this have persisted in academic and historian circles for decades. Maybe that is where Senator Conrad got the idea from and decided to use this as a political weapon. Maybe he saw it as a way of exposing to the larger public that Murchison favours some type of direct, and very expensive, action even after all these years. Otherwise I cannot really tell you why this erupted in such a vigorous and aggressive way. Politics, of course is politics. Conrad and Murchison hate each other. Both love to play mind games. So who really knows what Conrad is up to?"

"What about this Ralston guy, Andy? He didn't seem to do much to cool off Conrad's or Kendricks' jets. His comment about 'no matter the cost' seemed a bit out of line. Have you learned anything more about him?"

"Not really, Jay, but I will keep digging. I still think you need to let Senator Murchison in on this, Jay. I have known him for years and trust him explicitly. He has America's best interest at heart, always has. He is a good guy, Jay. Additionally he has the President's ear. After all he seems to be first in line to get the sitting President's endorsement for the upcoming campaign. He can help move this along. We really do need to move this along. Where are you on authentication?"

"Andy, I guess I finally agree with you. Let's get the Senator in on all this. Getting him in on it might also help me feel a bit safer. Tonight those two guys who I said have been following me cornered me in a pub. I was only able to wiggle away from them when some old friends showed up and, even then, likely only because those two didn't want to make a scene. I will be happy to put this behind me once and for all. What a couple of scary thugs those two are.

"By the way, tell the Senator that those two seem to have a real big ultra-right feel about them. The way they dress, the way they act, the way they look. You know my overly active imagination but I sense something here. You are more in tune with US politics than me but maybe there is even a direct connection with Conrad. How, I don't know, but it sort of smells like they are working for someone important and he could certainly fit the bill. Conrad bringing up Lincoln out of the blue like that sort of seals the deal for me.

"One of these two guys is named Gunnar or Gunner. I am not sure if that is his first or last name, and, judging from how proudly he adorned his jacket, he is from Idaho. He had a big patch or crest from Idaho on his jacket front."

"I have a colleague who teaches Criminology at the University who is also a retired FBI Agent. I will ask him, his name is Duncan, about any ultra-right movements in Idaho. Maybe he knows who this guy Gunnar/Gunner is. These right wingers seem to keep to pretty small and pretty insular groups. This buddy of mine has FBI contacts up the wazoo. If he can't identify this Gunnar/Gunner guy no one can. So, that's settled. What's next, Jay?"

"I meet with the expert tomorrow and I should definitely know, after that meeting, if the document is authentic. Once I get the final assessment, I will text you. I will text the single word YES if it is authentic. And if it is authentic I will also put a copy directly in an overnight courier to the Senator, Senator Murchison, not Senator Conrad, just to be clear. God help us if I sent it to the wrong Senator. Please text me Murchison's formal office address once we get off the phone.

"If you get a "YES" text from me tomorrow, try your damnedest to give Murchison a heads up as soon as you can. Even show him a copy of what I sent you last week if you think it wise. That way he will know what is coming.

"When I sat down with the expert, Thomas Rhodes his name is, earlier this week, I asked him to make me several genuine looking copies. If this document turns out to be not authentic, and once all this nonsense is behind me, I thought it might be fun to have copies for the kids. We are all family after all, us Lincolns and us Alexanders. Ha ha! Remember Honest Abe and I are cousins and you don't destroy family heirlooms even if they are forgeries.

"Much more importantly however, if it is authentic, I wanted to have backup copies too as I don't know what I may have to do before I get home. I might need to do a bit of bait and switch or some bartering while keeping the original secure."

"Sounds like we have a plan, Jay. I will look for a text from you tomorrow. I will clue the Senator in as soon as I can. He is not at his home in California right now but is in Washington. I know him well and have easy access to him and his Washington office staff. Oh, and Jay, please stay safe. I don't want anything to happen to my whisky sipping, Giants supporting, golfing buddy."

"Andy, I have a 6'6" ex-police officer with a mean straight arm looking out for me. Mutt and Jeff would best beware of him. And I can still ankle bite when necessary. It is a long story about my 6'6" ex-copper friend. I will fill you in on Ray later but I feel pretty safe, at least I do tonight. Talk soon, Andy. Bye for now. And look for my text tomorrow."

Important phone call done, I walk back into the sitting room to see three very curious faces staring at me.

Darcy says coyly, or is it sarcastically, "Talking to your girlfriend?" and then makes several silly kissing sounds, mwaw, mwaw, mwaw!

Before I can answer her, Ray says, "What's up? Is it about those two at the pub?"

I give them a short synopsis and add that I hope all will be resolved tomorrow. I tell them I need to go into town tomorrow and find out about the document's authenticity and, fingers crossed, end this one way or the other. I propose that either the whole escapade will turn out to be a non-event or I will have an important task to move forward with.

Ray asks me, "Do you need an escort for tomorrow? I know just the guy who can help. He may not be the sharpest tool in the shed but the guy can throw a mean left-right combination and is always up for a scrap."

I reply, "Yes please. That would be excellent. You can ride shotgun. Or rather you can drive shotgun. You know me and driving, or not driving, on the wrong side of the road."

Ray replies, "Then it is all settled. You and I will go into Alnwick tomorrow where you can see this book store expert. We'll get this sorted and put this shit behind you and maybe we can relax and have a few days of 'whack fuck'. I could use a few extra quid and you are always happy enough or crappy enough to let me take it from you."

'Whack fuck' is what Ray calls golf.

With that, Ray says "Magpie, my darling, it is time for our bunk. Let's go and leave these two to catch up." He winks at me, grabs Mags by the hand, and off to bed they go.

That just leaves Darcy and I sitting in uncomfortable silence which is only broken when she says, "Do you think they left us alone on purpose? My big sister Mags is always trying to play matchmaker and she never passes up an opportunity."

"I don't doubt for one minute that they left us alone on purpose. Sneaky aren't they," I add with a smile.

Darcy just sits there quietly and smiles back.

"Are you seeing anybody," I ask, with trepidation.

"Not currently, no I am not. In fact not too many dates of late, only three or four single dates since...well you know since when. No second dates, asked for or wanted. You?"

"Me, no not seeing anyone nor have I even been dating. Friends have tried a number of sly dinner party set ups but none have taken.

Truth be told, I have never even been tempted by these sneak attacks. My love life, sadly, has been very monk like."

"Do you miss it; you know the romance, the intimacy that you get from a relationship?"

"Me," I reply, "Not at all. In fact sometimes three or four minutes go by without me even thinking once about sex."

With that we both laugh but then an uncomfortable silence settles in again. Neither of us seems to know what to say next.

I learned a long time ago that when you expect rejection it is often best to really ask yourself "how bad can it be." Once you arrive at that answer, halve your view of the expected bad news. Once halved, then halve it again. That simple process usually takes one closer to the result you are likely going to get. It can still be bad but not the total disaster you so dread. This self-talk can often give us (read me) the where-with-all to take on the issue head on and deal with it, rejection be dammed.

The truth is we usually overestimate the bad news coming our way. This overestimate can lead us to hide and do nothing. I am sure all those self-help gurus have a fancy name for it but I just call it 'wimping out.'

I know I have something I really need to say to Darcy. I want to tell her I still have feelings for her. It is true! I do and I always will. But I am afraid that, if I tell her, I will be rejected quickly, directly and angrily and it will hurt. I recall all too well how we left things last time we spoke.

So again I ask myself, "How bad can it be?" We have already ended things, permanently it would seem, at least prior to tonight. She told me to "Fuck Off" when we last spoke. If I tell how I still feel and she tells me to bugger off again, 'How bad can it be?' We are already broken up. At this point we have no relationship anyway besides a polite promise to be 'friends.'

I am miserable but undeterred. So, I say to myself, "Suck it up, Princess," and finally, eyes fixed firmly on her, I manage to blurt out, "It is great to see you Darce and I really mean that. I have missed you. I do miss you. It has been way too long. I am so sorry the way we left it when we last spoke. I have a tendency, as you know, to be a bit insensitive with matters of the heart. I still think of you, of us, often. I am sorry and I would like to really be friends, if not even more than that."

Phew, I got that all out ....and without stuttering or crying.

To my great relief and to my absolute joy she expresses almost the exact same sentiments back to me. Again she apologizes for the "Fuck you, Jay" remark. She admits to still having feelings for me too and adds that she is sorry the way we ended it last time and sorry that we ended it, period.

It is amazing how much you can accomplish when you tell the truth. Who needs couples therapy when just telling the truth can often do the trick?

This is our great big Rom-Com moment. Or rather our 'meet cute' or, in actuality, our 're-meet cute.'

The next thing either of us knows we are in an embrace and kissing.

After a few moments of teenaged acrobatics, we suddenly stop. It seems, without saying anything out loud, we both instinctively decide to not move too fast. When we finally do gather ourselves and talk we agree it is best to move forward with one more try, cautiously and slowly, but caringly and hopefully.

After a few minutes or more of still awkward but heartfelt give and take we call it a night. I am not sure either one of us actually wants to go to our separate bedroom but propriety being what it is, the agreement we just made being set, off to separate beds we go. Plus we are also not exactly alone in this house.

"Night, Darce, see you in the morning."

"Night, Jay, don't let the bed bugs bite. Oh, and I hope you get more than three or four minutes of rest," she adds with a cheeky grin.

Maybe it is just my ego talking when I think neither of us really wanted to go to separate bedrooms. God, I hope it is not just my ego! Of course three or four minutes have gone by since she left.

I spend a rather restless night but for once it isn't about the Lincoln document and Shrek and his ultra-right pal, Donkey. Rather, over and over in my mind I play back the reunion with Darcy, the intimate and honest conversations we had, the things said and not said and, most importantly, where we go from here. I have to admit I am more than just a little hopeful. Despite some well-place apprehension I cannot wait to see what is in store for the two of us. I cannot wait to see her in the morning and see if we pick up as positively as we left off this evening.

9

Day Eleven

Everyone around here is an early riser, save me, but the noise and bustle gets me up before eight o'clock. After a round of coffee and/or tea (and of course Coke) we decide to wander the few blocks into the heart of the village, actually the heart is only one main street about 3 blocks long. We again take a long way around to make sure we are not being followed by Bert and Ernie. We decide to eat at the restaurant/bakery/grocery store/post office/card shop all in one...anyway you get what I mean. Hence, saying that the restaurant is multi-purpose is a bit of an understatement.

On the way I check my cell and find that, true to his word, Andy has texted me the Senator's office address in Washington.

At the restaurant/bakery/grocery store/post office/card shop the ladies each have a bowl of healthy home cooked oatmeal porridge with a cup of fruit on the side. Ray and I, being the true fitness freaks that we are, opt for the sausage breakfast baps, complete with a side of baked beans, all topped with a bit of brown sauce and washed down, at least for me, with my third cup of coffee of the morning. Ray is having his third Coke to wash down his bap.

He and I manage to survive the insults thrown our way by Mags and Darcy over our breakfast habits. Physiotherapists in particular don't recommend breakfast baps. But hell, I always say if you like it that way then have it that way. Actually I hardly ever say that but I often think it.

After breakfast and a brief walk along the beautiful beach, competing for space with the myriad of Labradors, Setters, Poodles and a surprising number of Dachshunds, we meander back to Mags' and Ray's house. First we stop by the cottage I rented as I need to attend to a few things including shaving off my 24 hour neck shadow, brushing my teeth and, not the least of all, changing my clothes and putting on another new golf shirt. This one I bought at Dunstanburgh.

That done, we go back to Ray's and Mags' to pick up Ray's pint sized SUV so the four of us can drive into Alnwick for my appointment with the document expert.

As we leave the cottage, Ray adds jokingly that it is nice to see me in another Barbour and Burberry outfit.

On the way back to the house to pick up the car we don't see either Sponge Bob or Square Head, but I am certain they are close by. Whether they are tracking us right now, however, we don't know. When walking back to the house we go a few blocks out of our way, including along another short forest trail, to make sure we aren't followed. At least that is our objective. We don't want them to know where Ray and Mags live.

We get to the bookstore just a few minutes before my appointed time at 10 AM. Those three wander in the book store amongst volumes old and new, vintage books, and manuscripts while I go to meet with the expert.

As I go into Thomas Rhodes' small and rather chaotic office, I am struck again at how one's preconceptions can fool one. There are vintage books and papers everywhere in the store but, instead of bound leather editions galore, it seems the chaos in this office is more about posters, magazines, comic books and soft covers. What is of value certainly has the capacity to change quickly these days.

When I think of an expert in authentication of vintage books, and even ancient manuscripts, I immediately think of someone like Dr. Jones Sr., the Sean Connery role from Indiana Jones and the Last Crusade. I imagine an older man, all tweedy, donning one of those hounds tooth bucket hats, with a thin grey beard or goatee, wearing wire rimmed bifocals, and perhaps with an unlit pipe in their mouth. Like Sherlock Holmes in repose.

When I first met Thomas Rhodes, three days ago, I was therefore quite surprised to meet an under 30's guy with longish hair, a tee shirt, torn and faded jeans, and ear phones hanging round his neck. I have admitted, on more than one occasion, to having an over-active imagination. So much for accurate stereo typing! At least today he was a wearing a Marks and Spencer sports jacket over his Aquaman tee shirt.

He greets me, all business, with, "Mr. Alexander, welcome back." No cordial small talk this time. "It is good to see you. I believe I have done a very thorough review of the document and have sought an expert second opinion from a highly qualified colleague in Newcastle. I drove down there myself to consult with him face-to-face. I am fully confident in what I am about to tell you."

"Please Mr. Rhodes, Thomas I should say, put me out of my misery. What conclusions have you reached? What do you think? Is it real?"

"I don't think it is real Mr. Alexander, I know it is real. This document is 100 percent authentic.

"I have aged the paper and it fits into the named time frame precisely. It is consistent with paper used in the mid-1860s. I won't bore you with the details of how we can confirm the aging of the paper but various production improvements in paper manufacturing and of supply were occurring quite rapidly in the nineteenth century. So much so that we can tie the paper to an almost specific year and production location. Such is the case with this document.

"That is it for the paper. As for the signature, my original assessment of the signature was 95 percent certain that it was Lincoln's.

Not being satisfied with 95 percent, I got opinions from three experts, the one previously mentioned colleague in Newcastle and two in the U.S., one in Boston and one in Philadelphia. To be safe I cropped a copy of the document and sent the signature portion only to all three. All agree it is Lincoln's signature. This raises my 95 percent assessment to 100 percent certainty that it was he, Abraham Lincoln, who signed it."

"Mr. Alexander", he goes on, "this is an incredibly interesting document. I suspect you do not intend to sell it, but if you do I can guarantee you the list of interested buyers would be a mile long. The dollar value would reach into the stratosphere. So, just out of curiosity, what are you going to do with it?"

"First off, thanks so much for all your work on this, Thomas. As for what is next I do not want to say right now. There are things to consider and things to do and I believe a proper order to do them in. I trust I can still rely on your total discretion on this. I have to implore you on this need for discretion. What is done, or might be done, with the document is best left free of rumour until it is decided by me and, more than likely, decided by others far better informed and far more important than I am."

"Say no more Mr. Alexander. You have my professional word and guarantee about confidentiality. You had said you also wanted three copies made", and handing them to me he adds, "Here they are."

With that he elaborates on the three copies and their amazing similarities with the original. They are so exact that I wouldn't know which was which if you gave me a 'ten times power' magnifying glass and a week to study them. He then takes the time to point out the one distinguishing feature between the original and the three copies. It is a small printer's mark that shows faintly on each of the three copies. You need to look very, very carefully to see it, and you have to know exactly where to look. But once you know where to look you can readily differentiate or distinguish copy from master.

We settle up the bill for the document authentication assessment and the three copies. The bill is steep but you always pay for quality and this guy is the best. Besides, I intend to have Senator Murchison reimburse me for the cost.

The bill settled, I then ask him where the nearest courier company is as I need to courier something to the United States. Actually I confide in him that I need to courier one copy of the document to the U.S. as soon as I can.

He informs me that it won't be necessary to look for a courier company. Because the book store has clients all over the world, as they often deal in very expensive vintage books and documents, and frequently with very demanding customers, they have rapid access to a twenty-four hour worldwide courier service.

He gives me an envelope to write the address on. I do so, put one copy of the document in the envelope, add a hurriedly scribbled note for the Senator, and hand it back to him. He gives me a rather surprised look when he sees the address on the envelope but, true to his word, he takes the envelope from me and assures me it will be delivered to the addressee tomorrow afternoon at the very, very latest.

He comments further, "It will likely be in the US this evening.

"Remember", he says, "It is just past dawn in the city in the USA where you want this delivered to, five hours difference to be exact. So we have lots of time. It should be there tonight, their time."

I feel very confident this will be done as promised, thank him most profusely and take the stairs down to the main floor to search for Darcy, Mags and Ray and see what they are up to. Before catching up with them, however, I take out my cell and text one single word to Andy, "YES", let out an extended sigh and, although I am not religious, say a little prayer.

Mags, Ray and Darcy are having tea, a Coke, and some type of delicious pastries in the book store coffee shop. It is really more like a restaurant than a coffee shop, complete with all kinds of homemade treats and tasty lunch dishes. Did I tell you how big this book store really is? It is one of a kind. Awesome! If you are ever in the area it is a must visit.

I sit with them until they are done snacking and together we decide to wander through town for a bit, up to the Castle and back, and then go for a quick drive up to Northumberland National Park for a short forest trail walk before we grab a late lunch at a small village called Wooler. We aim to be back at Ray's and Mags' by 4.00 or 4.30.

As we are wandering through town Darcy surprisingly takes my hand. Both Mags and Ray can be seen with self-satisfied smirks on their faces, those would be smirks in a good way.

We hadn't gone but two blocks when a car slows down to take a look at us. Staring at us from the windows of the car are Tweedle Dee and Tweedle Dumber. The bigger guy is driving and, as the car slows down, he grins at us and, in a rather threatening motion, runs his hand across his throat. He then honks the horn loudly and roars off at twice the posted speed.

As they speed away Ray and I both yell "ASSHOLES" loud enough to rival Kevin Kline angrily driving away in the movie 'A Fish Called Wanda'. If you have seen that movie you would be able to identify with Ray and my vocals at that moment. We even receive a brief round of applause from the locals on the sidewalk around us.

Now I know those two A-holes are still around, and clearly still stalking me, I realize that I need to do something before days end with the clearly precious original and the two remaining copies. I need to think on that. Where would they be safest? Where do I put them where nothing untoward can happen to them?

Assuming the Senator gets his copy by the end of today I hope I just have one or two more full days to put this whole mess behind me. Things feel a bit more promising anyway. Having the Senator on board will be a huge relief and having Ray continuing to watch my back is very reassuring as well.

After driving, actually racing, just a few more blocks down the road through Alnwick, Gunnar and Wyatt pull into a grocery store parking lot to make a phone call. Gunnar immediately dials up Tyrone. Tyrone doesn't answer until the fifth ring as it just 6.30am in Arlington, Virginian. Tyrone works out of his home in Arlington. To clarify for the rest of the geographically challenged, Arlington is just across the Potomac River from Washington D.C.

Tyrone doesn't recognize the number but answers anyway, "Who the fuck is this and do you know what fucking time it is? It better be fucking important."

As Tyrone deals with a lot of contacts who use pay-as-you-go phones it is not the least bit unusual that he doesn't recognize the number on many incoming calls.

"Tyrone, wakey, wakey. It's me, Gunnar. Sorry to disturb you so early but you wanted us to report in when we have something."

"Wakey, wakey yourself, asshole! Tell me you got this sorted," Tyrone snarls in reply.

"No, not yet, but I got good news. It seems our Canadian friend has a little side romance on the go. He and some woman were seen being all lovey dovey in Alnwick just now. This is the same woman he was with at the pub the other night. Seeing as he doesn't go anywhere without his pet gorilla accompanying him, I think we may have just found his weak spot.

"Wyatt and I are going to keep an eye on the broad. Snatching her will certainly be a good way to get Romeo to see things our way. We are going to hang around the village again today and tonight and see if we can find a place to nab her and if necessary her bosom buddy lady friend too. That should really shake things up."

"That sounds like the first smart thing you two have said in days. Keep me in the loop and good luck. By the way, you know that little chap you roughed up in that London book store? Rumour has it he didn't make it out of the hospital alive. So keep your heads down. You could be in the frame for this. And, if you do snatch the chick, don't fuck it up. Now leave me alone so I can grab another thirty minutes sleep before I have to get up and face the world."

Call over, and without even thinking about any extra sleep, Tyrone immediately dials Senator Conrad's direct line. He knows Conrad is a very early riser so won't have to apologize for the unscheduled 'wake-up call.'

"Senator, it's Tyrone. Before you ask, yes the call is safe. I just heard from Gunnar and Wyatt. It seems Alexander has a lady friend he is all gaga over. The boys are convinced that the way to this man's heart is, as usual, through his groin. So they plan on snatching the lady friend to get Alexander to barter. Fingers crossed we may know something by day's end."

The Senator already facing a busy day of fending off questions about the Texas preacher merely says, "Keep me informed," and hangs up with a thud.

Andy Hutchins is also an early riser. This morning, 8 hours behind his friend in England, he wakes up even earlier than usual. After crawling out of bed, already anxious about the document, he checks his cell for the message from me. Seeing the "YES" and wiping sleep from his eyes, while nursing a coffee he had to make from scratch (too early for the pre-set auto-timer) he calls Senator Murchison.

It has often been reported that Murchison never sleeps. Andy tells the Senator the document has been authenticated, rather, that it is indeed authentic. He knows from the text that the document, assumedly the original, is already on the way to the Senator's office and will be delivered by day's end. Still he feels the issue is too important to let lie even for half a day or so. He informs the Senator he is immediately forwarding a copy of what his Canadian friend had sent to him a few days back. He suggests the Senator look at the attachment as soon as it comes in. He assures the Senator that this will prepare him for the original once it arrives and give the Senator time to think about how to move forward from there.

Andy signs off by telling his friend, the Senator, that he will step away from this issue now and leave it for politicians and lawyers to deal with the fallout or whatever unfolds. He does, however, tell the Senator that if he, the Senator, needs anything from the historical perspective on this, that he, Andy, will be more than willing to help out.

Once off the phone, Andy immediately forwards to the Senator the e-mail and attachment he received from me several days ago. Finally the Senator will be able to see what all the fuzz is about.

Less than an hour and a half passes before the Senator is back on the phone with Andy.

"Andy, it is me, Jefferson. I have spent the last hour and a bit going over this document. Holy shit! This blows the walls off of Lincoln's already formidable legacy. The ramifications of this document are beyond anything I have seen in all my years in politics, and I have seen a lot. The monetary costs of this could be huge but pale by comparison to the social, economic and cultural ramifications. Given where the Country is at right now this might be the best, or worst, thing we can spring on the public. Some folks are going to stand up and cheer while others will go ape-shit. Violence will surely follow. This plays right into Conrad's hands. He will use this as a club to try and beat me and my colleagues into submission."

"Listen, Andy", he adds, "I need some time to mull this over and make a few phone calls. I will get back to you about what to do next with this and what to tell this Alexander guy friend of yours. If this was sent when this Alexander guy says it was sent, I assume I will have the original by early evening. And Andy, I know you wanted this to be over at your end, but I will still need your help for the next day or two, so please hang in there. I am sorry I can't cut you loose quite yet."

With that conversation done both hang up, leaving the Senator to contemplate next steps and Andy Hutchins to nervously wonder what he has gotten himself into.

Just an hour or so after the Senator and Andy had their last conversation, Ian Ralston is returning from lunching with the wife of a prominent journalist, the journalist being on assignment in the Middle-East, and the wife being on the prowl in D.C.

Ralston casually strolls into his elegant personal office in Washington. There is a large desk, several well-appointed and well stocked bookshelves, a sofa big enough to hold three guests, plus a rectangle table and chair set large enough to hold a gathering of up to ten people. There are several modern art prints on the walls and a very prominent framed photo of the sitting President, hung in a less than prominent place in the office. Ralston is impeccably dressed and perfectly groomed as usual.

Despite the quality of office a Communications Director seems to be entitled to, it pales in comparison to the opulent office a Senior Senator gets for themselves. It is into this opulent Senatorial office that Ralston is immediately summoned by his boss, Senator Murchison.

"Ian, please sit down. I need to show you something and I need your advice and assistance."

The Senator then shows Ralston the copy of the Lincoln document he received by e-mail attachment from California. He has been assured by his friend, Andy Hutchins, that the original document exists and may be on its way stateside soon.

Ralston reads it word for word, taking his time to do so. His expression changes several times as he looks through it. Is it shock, disgust, and anger that the Senator detects while watching Ralston read? For certain, the document has elicited a strong emotional reaction he has not seen from the normally calm and poised Ralston prior to now. This causes the Senator to moderately question his assessment of his new Communications Director and would-be Campaign Manager.

After Ralston puts it down, and it is obvious he has finished reading, the Senator continues, "What do you think? Every indication is that an authentic document could exist and, if it is so, the ramifications are enormous. Years of court cases for and against, billions of dollars spent or handed over, the potential of huge property transfers, lives disrupted, lives enhanced... it is staggering. And, of course, Lincoln could finally get his promises fulfilled."

Ralston replies, "If I were you, Senator, I would put that in the shredder and deny you ever saw it. I will back your story up. Making this public plays into the hands of the rumours Senator Conrad was talking about the other day. He will say you had it all along. Let it go! It will cause you and the country irreparable harm."

"That's certainly one tack to take, Ian. There are other options as well. We could try and action what Lincoln wanted his country to do. He was, after all, one of our greatest Presidents. Shouldn't we honour his wishes? Lord knows there are vast numbers of people in the country who deserve consideration for the egregious wrongs done to their ancestors.

"We could let the Supreme Court decide on the legality of the document, but that would mean a lengthy political battle that would make Roe vs. Wade look like a squabble between two neighbours over the height of a fence.

"We could, as always, bump it upstairs. Perhaps we should engage the White House and let the decision rest where it should, at the most senior level in the country."

"Let it go Senator. Get rid of it. Make sure it never sees the light of day. Addressing perceived past wrongs won't make them right. With an election on the horizon you don't want to be seen as the guy who ripped the South into shreds. Just let it go. That is my best advice."

"Thanks, Ian. I appreciate your input. I still need to think on this awhile. In the meantime this conversation, and what you just read here, does not get breathed outside this room. We need 100% confidentiality on this. Understood?"

"Understood, Senator."

After the Senator has said his piece to Ralston, the Senator looks down and begins to read what is in front of him. Without another word being uttered Ralston is clearly excused. As each day passes the Senator seems to be getting less impressed with his recent hire.

On his way back to his own office, Ian Ralston tells his assistant that he left something at the restaurant where he was lunching and he needs to go back and retrieve it. His assistant offers to go for him but he just shakes his head and says, "No you stay here. It is my forgetfulness and I need to pay for it. Besides, you are more important that I am," he adds, in what he thinks is self-deprecating humour.

Once out of the office, and having walked a block or so away, Ralston pulls out a burner phone and calls Tyrone Thorn.

Thorn answers almost at once with a sharp, "Yeah!"

"Tyrone, it is me, Ian. I just spent about fifteen uncomfortable minutes with the Senator and he showed me a copy of this phantom Lincoln document. Tyrone, it is real and it is really bad. It was/is a promise from Lincoln to take millions of acres of land away from decent, hard-working folks and give it to a bunch of f'ing people whose relatives apparently suffered years and years ago. We gave all those people homes and better places to live than did the shit hole African countries they came from? Whatever happened to the statute of limitations? What happened to forgive and forget? I think Murchison is considering getting this thing out in the open. I told him to let it die but his agenda is pretty clear. He wants to move the country to the Left and he just might seize upon this Lincoln promise as his chance to do so."

"Shit, Ian, I was afraid of this. Look, you stick to the Senator like glue and let me know if he even farts. In the meantime I have recently been in contact with Gunnar and Wyatt and told them to take whatever action is necessary to get the original and to stop this Alexander guy in his tracks. They seem to have found an Achilles heel with this Alexander guy and his love life so fingers crossed this will all be over soon."

Immediately after the call from Ralston, Tyrone calls Senator Conrad. After telling him, as always, that the call is safe, he updates the Senator on what Ralston has just told him. All the Senator says in reply is, "Just fix the fucking thing Tyrone," and slams the phone down.

While all this is unfolding stateside, we all get back to Ray's and Mags' a little bit after four o'clock in the afternoon after having enjoyed a walk up near Wooler and a nice lunch in that picturesque little market town. It is too late for Ray and me to walk down to the Alnmouth Village Golf Course and get in nine holes. It gets dark a bit earlier up here in the fall. None-the-less we do wander down to the club house/coffee shop anyway for a beer, a Coke and a chat with the locals. Mags and Darcy stay behind and likely engage in discussing the perceived weaknesses of Ray and I. Obviously it would be a short conversation given my near perfect personality and demeanour.

Based on our casual wandering down to the golf course and back, it seems that we are no longer worried about Beavis and Butthead or, at least, we are less concerned about covering our tracks. Ray's presence seems to have made them keep their distance. Ray still suggests it is best for me to stay at their house with them again tonight. I think this is partly out of worry for me being alone at the cottage but I also think it is part of Mags and his plot to reunite Darcy and me.

Staying at their house is not exactly a punishment. Their home is lovely. It is a postcard perfect two story cottage just on the edge of the village. Local estate agents would refer to a cottage like this in their adverts as 'Chocolate Box,' presumably because a picture of it would look perfect gracing the lid of a box of English chocolates.

The cottage has some kind of graded historical listing associated with it limiting renovations, not that it needs any. It is built of local stone with a small but charming walled garden in the back and a neat, detached, one car garage on the side.

If you were to search on-line for photos of the perfect English cottage you would likely see a picture of Ray's and Mag's, less the traditional thatched roof. By way of clarifying, the house does have a roof, it is just not thatched.

I believe the house used to be an old granary or school house. There are still several old granaries around. In years gone by, Alnmouth was famous for its export of local grains from the many farms in the area. It once had a vibrant and busy harbour for grain shipments but apparently the harbour, and even the course of the river Aln, was destroyed by a devastating storm many years ago. That was the end of the local grain shipments, at least from Alnmouth harbour.

Tonight we enjoy a fabulous roast of beef for dinner, complete with all the trimmings: Yorkshire pudding, gravy, mashed potatoes, mashed carrots and swede, all topped off with Sticky-Toffee pudding and several glasses of a good French red. Despite Brexit, the U.K. still has easy access to good French and Italian wines at near bargain basement prices compared to what we pay in Canada. Ray, of course, avoids any of this great wine and sticks with his usual Coke.

After clean-up is done by Ray and I, we all engage in some friendly banter and Mags forces us to play a game where you must choose between three well known characters and select, of the three, who you would marry, who you would date, and who you would dump. It is riotous fun which sees us break into near hysterics at times. The game comes to an abrupt end, however, when a less than cartoon savvy Darcy chooses Homer Simpson to marry instead of Ned Flanders. The other three of us laugh so hard that Darcy gets mad (I told you she has a temper) and refuses to play anymore. At least she doesn't react by saying "Fuck you, Jay."

Game done, snickering compressed by three of us, we all settle down comfortably to watch the news.

Not surprisingly, Ray and Mags beg off to go to bed early again and leave Darcy and me to our own devices. We chat for a while, which leads to more intimate conversation, which then leads to kissing. We kiss for a while and engage in some handsy behaviour (a couple of my old Fraternity Brothers at university about 100 years ago used to call this OB IB) and then, recalling our promises to take it slow, say an affectionate good night and go to our separate beds.

All I kept thinking as I try to get to sleep is that I wish this 'taking it slow' would go a lot faster.

10

Day Twelve

While it is an hour after midnight in Northumberland, and I am wistfully contemplating my love life in three to four minute increments, it is 8.00pm in Washington and 5.00pm back in California. Senator Murchison, knowing the seriousness of the consequences of this document becoming public without the requisite due care and context, has decided, despite his Communications Director's advice to the contrary, to share a copy with one of his very powerful White House connections. This connection is way up near the top of the government flagpole.

At first astounded by the document and its ramifications, this senior White House 'connection' and the Senator agree on a strategy. All strings are to be pulled forth-with to get the original document and myself into safe hands stateside. Both also agree that this has to be done hush-hush.

The Senator is tasked with calling his friend, Andy, and getting Andy to pass an important message to me. It seems their plan involves me being in Washington with the document in hand, and fast. They feel time is clearly of the essence. What is to happen to the document, and to me, after both are back in the Washington is either not discussed, not to be divulged, or not yet decided.

Fast asleep and dreaming about green fields, snow-capped mountains, rushing steams, and a beautiful English girl, strangely named Heidi, I am cruelly awoken by my cell phone on the bed side table. Cursing to myself and to this disturbance to my dreams, I pick up the phone with a groggy but simple, "Hello. Who is it?"

To my surprise it is Andy.

"God, Jay, I am sorry to have to wake you. I know it is only 3.00am there but things are moving really quickly back here. The Senator, Murchison that is, has the document you couriered to him and feels the need to advance this really quickly. Are you awake and listening, Jay, because this is terribly important?"

"Yes, Andy", I snarl in return, "I am listening. This is terribly important," I add with more than just a mild hint of sarcasm in my voice. Sometimes I can be a real asshole!

Ignoring my snide attitude, Ray continues, all business like, "Okay, good, I have your attention. The Senator has read the document and realizes its importance. Not to be lost in any of this, of course, is the press conference held the other day by Conrad and how to spin all this now that rumours are true. Senator Murchison has quickly shared all this with his important, seriously important I hear, contacts at the White House. Yes, Jay, at the White House.

"This is what I, or rather what they, the Senator and the White House, need you to do. They want you to get on the first London bound train you can out of Alnmouth. Get off at the train station in Peterborough. As I am you sure you already know every southbound train on that route stops at Peterborough. Someone will meet you at the Peterborough train station. I assume they will be holding a sign near the exit gate but, no matter what, I assume you can easily identify the contact or they can easily ID you. This person will drive you directly to Stansted Airport. Stansted Airport is a little over an hour away from Peterborough by car.

"The person who picks you up and drives you to Stansted will drop you off at the airport with another contact there. All this has been prearranged. That contact will, in turn, get you to a government jet that will fly you direct to Washington, D.C.

"Once you touch down in D.C. it has been arranged for you to quickly clear customs. You will then be handed over to a further contact. This person will take you by car directly to the White House.

"At the White House you will be met by the Senator and whomever his 'very important' White House contact is/are. I then assume they will go over all this shit with you and what role they may have for you going forward. Phew, I realize that is quite a mouthful. Have you got all that?"

Andy then gives me a phone number to call if anything goes amiss on my travels south to Peterborough. I immediately add that number to my list of cell phone contacts.

Awake now, and keeping with my underappreciated sense of humour, I say to Andy, "What was that first thing again?"

This is met with the predictable. "Fuck you, Jay." Where have I heard that before?

Getting hold of myself, I then insist Andy go over all this again slowly so that it is clear. We do this twice more to be certain.

I reconfirm that the phone number I entered in my cell phone contacts is correct. I then tell him that there is an early morning train from Edinburgh to London that stops at Alnmouth. It departs Alnmouth at 7.00am and I will be on it. Next, I advise him the train should take a little under three hours to get to Peterborough. Finally, and somewhat grumpily, I remind Andy that we are quite far north of Greater London up here in Alnmouth, so it is not just a twenty minute jaunt down the road. I remark that if this is all so rush-rush and important why didn't they bring the government plane up to Newcastle which is less than forty miles from here? After Andy responds that he doesn't think the White House has much of a clue about U.K. geography we proceed to wrap this conversation up.

"Great," he adds. "We have a plan. I will let the Senator's office know that they should expect you in Peterborough by about

10.00am and to Stansted Airport by about 11.00. Sorry to dump all this on you so quickly, buddy, but this is important. Duh, I guess you already know that. We can catch up once you get this White House business done. The first whisky is on me."

I reply, "The first case of whisky is on both you and the Senator. Nothing but single malt aged 12 years or older will do, the peatier the better."

"Oh, and one more thing," Andy adds, "I heard back from my friend Duncan, at Stanford. Duncan is the guy who is teaching criminology. You know, the guy I told you who has FBI contacts up the wazoo. He got back to me yesterday and his contacts told him that they are pretty sure your round-the-clock shadow Gunnar/Gunner is a guy named Gunnar Nielsen, that's Gunnar spelled with an N-A-R not an N-E-R. This Gunnar is an ultra-right fanatic who is connected to some shadowy organization called the Brothers of Freedom.

"The Brothers of Freedom is a group started in the U.S. midwest about ten years ago and has spread country wide, not in great numbers, but still large enough and single-minded enough to be of concern. They are white supremacists who would like nothing better than to go back to the way things were prior to the Civil War. Oh, and they support immediately discontinuing all immigration except for white Western Europeans.

"They claim they are free citizens and can do pretty much whatever they want. They think taxes are illegal and demand the right to carry weapons whenever and wherever they please. They were prominent as vigilante types in some of the 'Black Lives Matter' protests and active participants in Charlottesville. A lot of them are ex-military so are skilled in combat tactics and subterfuge and hence viewed as extremely dangerous.

"This Gunnar travels in pretty tight circles with a number of other guys linked to the same or similar organizations. It seems he is inseparable from another racist named Wyatt Bing. They are seldom seen apart. Wyatt Bing is likely the other goon who has been trailing you over there.

"Apparently this Gunnar Nielsen guy, and his pal Bing, were both bounced from the ROTC. I was unable to learn why. They both immediately reenlisted and served in the Middle East. This Gunnar was dishonorably discharged. I cannot find out why Bing left or was discharged. Rumours have it that they still travel around telling everyone they graduated with honour from the ROTC and served, with distinction, as officers. They cannot be counted on to say anything even closely resembling the truth.

"These two, and their 'Brothers,' are in constant contact with a guy in Arlington, Virginia, named Tyrone Thorn. This Thorn guy is well connected in supremacist circles as well, and is believed to be Numero Uno in this Brotherhood and, if not number one, he likely reports directly to number one.

"The FBI has these 'Brothers', especially this Thorn guy, under constant watch. I don't know if that includes wire-tapping and 24-hour surveillance but it is apparently quite thorough scrutiny. Duncan is going to get me a photo, or photos, of the three of them and I will attached the photo(s) to a text I will send to you once the photos are received so you can compare faces with your two shadow companions over there.

"Again, sorry about dumping all this on you, Jay. I best let you go as you have things to do. Bye for now buddy. Good luck and God speed."

I respond in kind and hang up, nervous but excited and determined.

Having received my marching orders, and aware of the tight time frames, I decide the best person to help me now, decided mostly with my heart (with influence from other body parts), is Darcy. Trying to be sure not to wake up Ray and Maggie, I sneak quietly into the bedroom Darcy is in and gently nudge her hoping to wake her up.

With a third gentle push she wakes up and, a bit startled, looks up and me and says, "Not on your life buddy, now go back to bed."

I cannot help but smile at this but, putting the smile behind me, I quietly and quickly fill her in on what is up. Together we decide not to wake up Ray or Mags. Instead we decide that she will drive me to the rental cottage where I can pack my bag and pick up what else I need for my rapid fire return to the U.S. She has her car with her at Ray's house.

We decide that once I have done my quick packing at the rental cottage she will then take me to the train station and see me off.

While she is getting dressed, I go on-line and book my train ticket to Peterborough. Assuming the White House has the money and owes me big time, I book a first class train ticket. I also compose a cryptic note for Ray and Mags telling them, "All is in order. No need to worry. I am on the train to London and from there I just need to head stateside fast. This hurry-up trip is connected with the 'document' and I need to meet someone there ASAP". I leave this note in the kitchen

To be sure, I also text the same message to Ray, adding to this text that Darcy will fill them in later once she is back from the train station.

Checking myself in the mirror I then remember that I need to get dressed too. Finally, dressed and messages written/sent, off we go to the rental cottage.

We arrive there promptly, not trying to conduct evasive measures this time. I do my packing very quickly as not a lot is required. I travel light. I change again, this time into the most Washington presentable clothes I have with me, still pretty causal as I was not expecting to go to the White House when I left home 11 days again. I then ask Darcy to make sure my golf clubs are shipped back home and assure her I will repay her so she won't have to sell a kidney to pay for the shipping costs.

The White House may be a priority but how could I ever forget my golf clubs. The things we grow to love, but golf clubs? Really?

Before we depart for the train station, I remove my 9 iron from my golf bag and give it to Darcy for her to put in the car in case she needs to defend herself or defend me. You never know who we might run into on our way to or at the train station. And I won't have Ray with me to run interference.

We arrive at the station about fifteen minutes before the train's 7.00am departure. The station is small with just two tracks passing through, one set northbound and one set southbound. The ticket office and waiting room are both on the southbound side. There is a parking lot on each side, neither of them particularly large.

Darcy parks in the parking lot closest to the northbound platform. It is only a two minute walk to cross over the overhead walkway and catch my train south. We are standing there hugging like a couple of love struck teenagers when, looking across the tracks to the southbound platform we see Fatman and Robin staring back at us. It looks like we may be at a stalemate but Darcy and I are not stupid and we already have an escape plan all worked out.

Just as those two goons spot us and begin their menacing smirks, with the bigger one duplicating the cross the throat motion, the northbound train pulls into the station. This northbound train is destined for Edinburgh. It is always a quick stop at Alnmouth, it not being the busiest stop on the way north. In fact it is the briefest.

There is hardly anyone waiting on either platform. In fact there is talk the station may soon close permanently due to low traffic.

When the northbound train pulls away, Fatman and Robin look across the tracks and see I am gone. Did I get on the train to Edinburgh I am sure they wonder? Only Darcy is standing there. She pauses for a few seconds, gives a small wave, and heads for her car.

My two 'would be' shadows take off full tilt to get in their car, presumably, to chase the train north and get to Edinburgh's Waverly Station before my train gets there.

Once the two of them have cleared the platform, racing toward their rental car, I climb out of the back of Darcy's car, grab my small suitcase and backpack, give Darcy a big hug and kiss and dash across the overhead walkway. The southbound train to Peterborough, and its final destination of London King's Cross, is just pulling in. As I turn to walk, actually run, to catch my train, Darcy said to me, "Be careful. Let me know once you get to Washington. Oh, and one more thing, I think I love you."

Don't ask me why but just for a moment I contemplate replicating Han Solo from the Empire Strikes Back and simply say, "I know." But, given our recent difficulties, I am astute enough to know that would be unwise, even if very humorous. Instead, I man up, let my true feelings out and reply "Well, I know that I love you." With that I am gone, in a full sprint, to catch the train.

When on board, I take a forward facing window seat on the left side of the train. Who wants to go 200 plus miles facing the wrong way? As the train slowly departs the station I look out the window and see Darcy standing there and watching, and then she offers me a small wave.

11

Comfortable in my first class seat, waiting to enjoy a free breakfast, and contemplating, not for the first time, that this will soon be all behind me, I finally start to really relax. The train hasn't gone far, perhaps only about fifteen minutes out, when my cell phone rings. I am so happy to see it is from Darcy. She misses me already.

I answer with a sing-song, "Well, hello stranger. Long-time no see. Miss me already?"

To my dismay, and ultimately to my horror, the voice at the other end of the call says, "Well, hello asshole. Yes it has been a long-time no see. Do you miss us too?"

Before I can gather my wits and respond the voice on the line says, "In case you haven't figured it out already this is your old friend Archie, or am I Jughead. You were not very specific about who was who when you were entertaining us, in the pub, with your fabulous sense of humour. You see, asshole, we are not as dumb as you apparently think we are. We are highly respected ROTC alumni, suma cum laude and all that shit. No army for us any more though. It seemed the Military didn't want us after all. Seems while we were out of the country the Brass decided we were a bit too mean to the ragheads. Fuckin' Taliban and their damn women.

"Anyway enough history. We saw right through your little hidden train trick at the station. It just took us a few minutes to drive around to the other parking lot and pick up a package. You see some nice looking broad was standing there waving just waiting for us to invite her into the trunk of her own car. She wants to say hi by the way; at least I think that what she is trying to pound out by Morse Code from back there in her trunk. Want to say hello?"

"If you two pricks touch her I will...."

"You will what? You ain't gonna do shit until I tell you what to do. So listen up as I am now going to tell you exactly what you are going to do.

"You are going to get off the train in Newcastle. Then you are going to grab a cab, rent a car, hop on the next train, hitch hike or whatever you deem necessary and get back here as soon as you can. The faster you get back to Alnmouth the less time your lady spends locked in her trunk.

"We will be waiting for you at that cute little rental cottage of yours. Don't try anything funny and don't bother to call for reinforcements as your lady friend isn't at the cottage, and won't be. You see she is hidden away in a nice quite spot, resting comfortably in her trunk. God, I hope there is enough air for her, so you better hurry."

"What is it you want asshole?" I blurt out.

"This is quite simply a swap Romeo, the girl for the Lincoln document. So hurry and come alone with no fucking about. If we see anything untoward we will simply disappear and you will likely never know where your sweetie has been stowed. However, before we do disappear, we may have to pay a brief visit with your lady friend one final time as Jughead, as you call him, seems to have taken a real shine to her."

"But, but..."

"Bye for now asshole, see you real soon," and he ends the call abruptly.

I am in full-blown panic mode. Luckily, given the dire warning about the need to hurry, we are only about ten minutes out of Newcastle. But how to get back to the cottage quickly?

A fast internet check shows at least an hour before the next train heads north. I know all about buses in this part of the world and, even if one was immediately available, they stop at every dinky little hamlet between Newcastle and Alnmouth. A cab, I can take a cab. There are always a few waiting at Newcastle Station and I am flush with English pounds.

As soon as the train comes to a full stop I run out of the station as if being shot out of a cannon. Luckily, despite the rush, I remember to grab my backpack and my suitcase from the overhead rack.

What I see right in front of me is what I think is a local taxi cab. The engine is running but there is no sign of the driver. Clearly he or she is off grabbing a quick coffee or helping someone with their heavy luggage. So, without thinking things through, I take the cab. I mean I literarily 'take the cab.'

I hop in the vehicle, toss in my bags, and take off before I even have time to remember I hate driving on the wrong side of the road. Despite that, I bet I lay about 100 yards of rubber... black smoke everywhere. Surprising as the cab is an automatic. Fortunate too that it is an automatic as I haven't driven a standard transmission since I got drunk in high school about 35 years ago and boosted a friend's ride.

Taxis in the U.K., especially those from smaller towns and villages, often do not have any obvious distinguishing markings that show they are taxis. So I also have that going for me. Once the call goes out about 'grand theft auto' at the Newcastle Train Station I won't stand out like a sore thumb when I hit the A-1.

I know the A-1 goes straight up to Alnwick so it will be easy to get to the cottage from there. I know it is less than forty miles from the airport so, if I step on it, I can get there in thirty to thirty-five minutes. I don't hold back on the gas pedal. Oddly, I am in such a panic that I don't even think about which side of the road I need to be on or which side of the car the steering wheel is on. I just fly. The transition to right hand drive comes naturally when you don't dwell on it and when you are shitting your pants in terror.

I just soar, full tilt, out of the Station heading for the A-1, that is until I come to the first roundabout. We have lots of roundabouts in Canada now but very few of them have two lanes and very few of them have so many f'ing exits. And, of course, you don't enter any of them by merging to your left.

In I go and I end up circumnavigating that sucker three times before I find the proper exit lane and the proper exit. What's that I said before about centrifugal force? I am going so fast around this damn thing that when I exit I am sure my speed doubles. I am almost airborne as I leave the roundabout and head toward the A-1.

Once on the A-1 it is a relatively easy drive up. Maybe I can learn to enjoy driving over here after-all, just not right now.

The hardest part is trying to dial Ray on my damn cell phone while I am flying along at about 75 miles an hour. I know what Archie and Jughead said about coming alone but there is no way I am going into that cottage without back-up and, as I am certain they are desperate to make the trade, I am sure they won't bugger off without the document in their grubby little hands. And I know, without Darcy safely in my arms, they won't get what they so desperately want.

With only half an eye on the road, while steering the car with two fingers, I fumble through the various buttons on the cell phone trying to make a call to Ray. Through some minor miracle I finally hit the right buttons, in the right order, and the call goes through. Ray answers almost immediately.

"Holy shit, Jay, you left in a hurry. I got your note and your text. So where are you? Half way to London? I hope those SOB's in America paid for a first class rail ticket."

"Ray, Ray, listen to me, please just listen to me! I don't have time to explain everything but those two goons who have been following me have grabbed Darcy. They have got her stowed away somewhere and want to trade her for the document I just had authenticated. I am in a car heading up the A-1 right now and should be back in Alnmouth in less than 30 minutes.

"Stay where you are as I am coming directly to your place and will pick you up before I have to meet those two pricks face to face. And Ray, don't invite any of your ex-copper buddies along. These guys mean business and we need to get this swap done without Darcy getting hurt. If we panic them there is no telling what they may do or if they will ever tell us where they have Darcy hidden."

"What the fuck Jay? Are you sure Darcy is safe? And," he adds in shock, "Are you really driving a car?"

"Enough chit-chat Ray. Just do as I say and stay put until I get there, please buddy. I gotta go now."

With that said I hang up and concentrate on my driving, actually my speeding. It doesn't even dawn on me that I have someone waiting for me at Peterborough train station and a flight to D.C. on my schedule. That is the last thing on my mind at the moment. Paramount of course is Darcy and secondarily is listening for sirens behind me seeing as I have just committed the grand theft of a vehicle. Police do not seem to take too kindly to that and, if I get pulled over, what happens to Darcy?

Managing to steer the car up the A-1 is done easily and quickly. I do have to suffer through one more roundabout before I can access the final five miles or so into Alnmouth. This roundabout I deal with like an old pro and again exit at twice the entry speed. Good old centrifugal force.

I really have a handle on this driving on the wrong side now. However I soon realize that narrower country roads, with traffic coming at me less than a foot or two to my right, is a bit more nerve-racking than the A-1 was. Most of these roads have no shoulders to speak of, at least not by North American standards. I guess that is what happens when 1000 year old donkey tracks get covered with blacktop.

I manage to cover the last five miles in near record time and would have bettered any record if it weren't for the odd local farmer going at half the speed limit. I don't recall ever before passing so many vehicles in such a short time. It is amazing how quickly cars (and tractors) will get out of your way when you approach them at seventy-five miles an hour, from behind, while really laying on the horn.

Finally, less than thirty-five minutes after I left the Newcastle train station, I pull up in front of Ray's and Mags' house. Before I can get out of the car Ray is already climbing in to the passenger seat.

"Jesus, Jay, what kind of a mess have you got yourself and Darcy into? How dangerous are they two assholes anyway? What exactly do they want you to do? What will they do when they see me with you? What's the plan?"

Before I can answer he asks one more question. "Where the fuck did you get this car from? This is a local taxi? Did you steal a fuckin' taxi? Jay, I am an ex-copper with a stellar reputation in this town. What are you dragging me into? First you drop Darcy in the glue and now me!"

That tiny little new fact about a stolen car, and Ray's awareness of the need for a plan, leads us to pause for four or five minutes, put our heads together, and devise our strategy to rescue Darcy while also keeping me out of an English jail (or is it gaol)?

First I drive the taxi up a dead end alley in town and leave it there. I take £500 out of the wallet-like billfold I keep in my backpack and leave the money in the glove box of the taxi. I hurriedly scribble out a note expressing my apologies, saying it was a life or death situation. I add on the note that I have left £500 in the glove box for the inconvenience and have left the keys on top of the tire on the rear passenger side. I then lock the car and place the keys in the hiding spot.

We agree that Ray will place a call to the owner of the cab once Darcy is safe. We suspect the car I swiped may not actually belong to a taxi company, but just a lone guy who runs a one man taxi service in a small village. That is common over here in the U.K. The £500 should ease his/her concerns and negate any prolonged international police pursuit.

On the call Ray will explain where the car is, how to find it, and where the keys and £500 can be found. Of course he will make the call from a phone box if there still is one of those legendary red boxes left in the U.K. In any event when he calls, and from whatever phone he makes the call from, he will ensure it is anonymous and not traceable back to us.

We decide that we will both walk directly into the rental cottage, side by side, but that we will not engage in any shenanigans, at least until we are certain that Darcy is safely within our reach.

Using Ray's SUV we then drive directly to the rental cottage, a mere few minutes away. No trying to disguise our trail this time.

The door to the cottage is unlocked and, as we walk in, we are immediately greeted by the bigger of the two, Gunnar.

"What the hell buddy? I told you to come alone. What the fuck is this guy doing here? Do you want us to make your lady friend disappear forever?"

"Look," I snap back, "You got your backup, I got mine. His being here doesn't change the deal. The deal is the document for my lady and that is exactly what I intend to get done. If you have a problem with that then I am glad I have my buddy with me and we will do what we need to do right now to squeeze what we need out of both of you."

This is pretty brave of me seeing as I wouldn't have much to offer in a street fight. I am about pissed enough to step in to these two right now. However I am also wise enough to know that a fist fight won't safely get us Darcy back nor ensure I am left standing in one piece after the donnybrook.

The other guy, Wyatt, Gunnar refers to him just now as Wyatt, pipes up, "Alright, alright, settle down boys. Beating the shit out of you two assholes might be a lot of fun but won't get us anywhere. Let's stick with the plan. Give us what we want and you will get your lady back. Simple as that! No harm no foul."

"You get dick all from us until I see my friend," I reply angrily.

Gunnar then steps back in, "Do you think we are stupid? I would think that the way we handled your cute little disappearing act at the train station should have proved to you that we ain't stupid. So let me tell you exactly what is going to happen. No options. No negotiation.

"Only we know where your lady friend is and we are quite prepared to tell you where she is but, until we have the document in our hands, you don't get to know shit.

"You hand over the document to us now. We head out getting as far away from this fucking place as we can in the next 2 ½ hours. In the meantime you sit quietly by your cell phone. I already have your number. In precisely 2 ½ hours we will call you and tell you where she is. You can then go off and retrieve her and receive a hero's welcome. Kiss, kiss.

"By then we will have scarpered off and gotten ourselves out of this fucking shit-ass country before you can call in the coppers and get any APBs out on us. That's the deal. Take it or leave it. Are you in or not?"

Knowing we really don't have any realistic alternative we reluctantly agree. I go back out to the car and get the second copy of the document. Remember how official these copies look and that these two university dropouts won't be able to tell they are getting a copy. In fact, given the circumstances and their egos, I doubt they will even consider what I give them might not be authentic.

Once back from Ray's car I hand the copy over to them. In the same jittery motion they hand me the keys to the trunk of Darcy's car. I make certain they have the correct cell phone number for me. We agree on, actually they dictate to us, the exact time they will call to tell us the location of the car. We, in turn, promise not to sic the local constabulary on them (at least until Darcy is safely in hand). After we have Darcy securely in hand, and out of harm's way, all bets are off. Then we will do our utmost to ensure these sons of bitches get what they deserve.

With their ultimatum agreed to, they bugger off and we sit nervously waiting and praying that the call will come by the end of the agreed 2½ hours.

With the document they so desperately wanted now in their hand, out of the cottage and quickly on the road to Newcastle, Wyatt takes out his phone to call Tyrone and let him know all is fine.

Gunnar asks, "Who the fuck are you calling?"

All excited and pumping adrenaline, Wyatt replies, "I am going to phone Tyrone and let him know we have the document and we can all rest easy. None of those black sons-of-bitches are gonna get a thing out of whatever it was Lincoln promised them. We won and I want to let Tyrone in on the celebration."

"It is 4.00 in the morning in Arlington, Virginia, you fucking idiot. Let's just concentrate on getting to the airport in Newcastle in one piece. I want to get out of this bum-fuck country as soon as we can. We have a plane to France to catch just after 11.00 this morning. Once we are on that plane we won't have to worry about coppers, about those two assholes, or about Tyrone and the Senator riding our asses for not getting this thing done sooner. We can rest easy.

"If you want to tell Tyrone, then send him a text but make it short and sweet. Just send him a text and say 'job done.' Now shut the fuck up and let me get us to the airport. Our flight leaves at 11.15."

Looking over at his pouting passenger, Gunnar spits out, "Stop moping. If you want to be more wordy just text, 'job done, document destroyed, all good, now on our way home'. There is really no more to say than that anyway."

With that conversation done, text sent, and Wyatt chastised, the two continue to drive the forty miles or so down to the Newcastle airport to catch their plane.

After a few minutes of quiet reflection Gunnar decides that to stop Wyatt from pouting maybe they do need to celebrate their success. They talk it through and decide they will stay in Paris for a few extra nights of some well-deserved R&R, or as Wyatt puts it wine, woman, more wine, more woman, more wine, more women and then song.

That decision made they next contemplate just leaving Darcy where she is and whatever happens to her happens to her. The two have a very intense exchange about this. It is actually Wyatt Bing who is the more adamant that they do make the phone call. He has always been close to his mother and two sisters and, despite being a tough SOB when required, he also holds a soft spot for what he refers to as the 'fairer sex.' He was not so considerate of the 'fairer sex' when serving in Iraq and Afghanistan but he is much more mindful here.

Ultimately the two agree that, as their task has been successfully completed, they will honour the agreement and phone me just before their plane leaves and tell me, and my gargantuan body guard, the location of Darcy and her car.

Some fifteen minutes before boarding their flight out of Newcastle Gunnar Nielsen calls me and, after a few well aimed insults, divulges the location of Darcy's car and, of course much more importantly, Darcy.

Assigned mission completed, they decide they will stay incognito, or in more formal military terms 'maintain complete radio silence,' until they get back to D.C. in a few days' time. No calls home, no incoming call accepted, just freedom to do what they want. They feel they deserve the rest and they don't want any more flack, distractions, or shitty assignments from Tyrone or from the Senator to interrupt their down time.

Just before last call for boarding call, Wyatt sends one more text to Tyrone, this time saying, "Job done and dusted. We are going to lie low until we get back stateside. We are going into radio silence. Dumping this phone now. We will contact you in three or four days once we are safely back in the good old USA. Sayonara for now."

Shortly before 11.00am, less than four hours after getting on the train to Newcastle, my phone rings. We are in Ray's and Mags' house in Alnmouth. The three of us have been sitting here on pins and needles hoping for a call to come in soon and fearful a call might not come at all.

Ray and I have also had to endure various insults and accusations from Mags about how we could be so stupid, how we could put Darcy in such danger, and how I could have gotten into this mess in the first place. The word dickhead was tossed my way more than once, actually I likely heard it ten or twelve times. A few distraught tears were also shed. Mags and Darce are not just sisters but best friends!

I snatch up the phone on the first hint of a ring. Before I can even let out a sound Gunnar starts in.

"Well hello asshole. Hope you and your little buddy, Paul Bunyan, have had a nice morning. Despite my better judgement, and only because my little pal Jughead likes women, we have decided to tell you where you lady is."

He then gives me a clear description of exactly where to find the car.

Before signing off he adds, "And don't try any funny business with the coppers. We are already on an outbound flight and should be landing in a non-extradition treaty country before you can say Jack Robinson. We will be out of your hair forever, not that it wasn't pure joy doing business with you. It has truly been a pleasure...NOT! Our business now having been done there is not much else left to say except have a nice life and give the little lady a kiss from Wyatt."

With one more sarcastic, "Sayonara assholes," he hangs up.

I have Mags and Ray on the speaker and they both know instantly exactly where the car is. It is in a secluded but accessible place, an old abandoned granary site just outside Alnmouth proper. It seems that because my two adversaries had to deal with two cars, and also get me on the phone before I got to Newcastle, they couldn't hide Darcy's car too far afield. A lucky break for us as amongst our worst fears was that the car would be hidden in remote area miles away from Alnmouth.

Despite the fact that we are really less than ten minutes from where the car is we literally sprint out of the house and into the SUV and are speeding on our way. Ray is driving now like I did earlier today, madly, pedal to the metal, regardless of roads signs, other traffic, fear of police cars, or of the relatively short distance we need to travel.

We reach the hiding spot in a mere matter of minutes. Screeching to a halt beside Darcy's car, I leap out, keys in hand and run to the trunk in full panic mode. I fumble with the keys and try three or four times to get the right key into the lock. Finally an exasperated Mags grabs the keys from me, tosses one more dickhead comment my way, puts in the correct key, and flings the trunk open. Darcy, having heard someone outside, had already commenced pounding on the inside of the trunk, and screaming like a banshee for help, while all this slapstick comedy was going on outside.

After a few startled seconds of adjusting to the light, and trying to recognize who has rescued her, if indeed it is not her two captors having returned, she realizes it is me, it is Ray, and it is Mags. She agilely springs from the truck despite having her hands tied behind her back, a feat of athleticism we might all have laughed about or admired in difference circumstances.

Following several frantic and unsuccessful attempts we finally manage to get her hands free. She throws her arms around me, says "thank God" several times and immediately breaks into tears. This joyful reunion is short lived, however. She next proceeds to pound her fist into my chest over and over, sobbing uncontrollably, while cursing me using language that would make even the most seasoned sailor blush.

We finally get her calmed down; actually we don't, Mags gets her calmed down. After a few more moments of unbridled verbal assaults Mags takes Darcy back to their house. Ray and I follow them in his SUV. It was made abundantly clear to me that Darcy was not going to get into a car with me any time soon.

Ray drives back home much more slowly than the way he drove out as we are both quite leery of the type of reception we will get back once we get back. Sheepish is a good word to describe us.

Back at the house we try and talk over what has happened, why it happened and, unfortunately for me, who was to blame for it all. It isn't a happy exchange of views.

More tears, a lot of yelling and a lot more dickhead remarks aimed my way. I think I hear a couple more of the now all too familiar, "Fuck you, Jay," utterances as well. I am left feeling overwhelmed, thoroughly chastised, very remorseful but, in equal measure, exceedingly grateful now that Darcy is fine.

Here I sit, a typical Canadian, happy, yet remorseful and apologetic all at the same time. I am sorry, eh!

12

While I am in the midst of receiving these serious recriminations my cell phone rings rather unexpectedly. Oh great, perfect timing I think. Who could want me at the juncture?

When I answer, it is an unfamiliar, yet decidedly American, voice that starts out with, "Is this Mr. Alexander?"

"Yes," I respond with considerable curiosity all the while thinking to myself, "This isn't the best time to call, buddy."

"Mr. Alexander, I was just wondering where the hell you are. I am waiting for you at the Peterborough train station and, despite a couple of trains having come and gone, I have not seen hide or hair of you. They tell me this is a pretty urgent situation so I hope you have a damn fine excuse for holding us up and for holding up the White House. Care to fill me in on what is going on?"

Now it all comes racing back to me. So worried about Darcy, and so caught up in the quarrel with Archie and Jughead, I had forgotten about my promise to be on a plane to D.C.

I blather out some kind of excuse about a family emergency and tell the guy I am stuck in Alnmouth.

"Alnmouth? Where the hell is Alnmouth and how in the hell am I supposed to get you to Stansted from there? Folks are waiting for you both here and back in D.C."

I tell him that Alnmouth is about forty miles north of Newcastle. Before I can put forward any reason for not keeping my engagement in Washington, he says to me; "Listen son, you make sure you are at the airport in Newcastle in forty-five minutes. I will have the pilot bring the plane up there from Stansted and pick you up. The pilot can take you directly to Washington from there."

He then adds, "Why in the hell didn't we pick you up from there in the first place? We would have been on our way hours ago. Somebody didn't tell somebody something they needed to know. God-damn Washington bureaucrats couldn't find their asses with two hands and a flashlight. Just get your butt down to that airport, Newcastle Airport just to be clear, and do it pronto, understood?"

I try and insert a word or two but he cuts me off and says, "Never mind son! Just get your God damned ass to the Newcastle Airport, STAT!"

I am faced with a dilemma for which the resolution, sadly, is all too clear. I need to take a few minutes and make my peace with Darcy and then get my ass to Newcastle. I contemplate for a few minutes driving myself back in the cab but better judgement prevails. Ray says he better take me. I grab my small suitcase and my backpack and head for his pint sized SUV.

On the way out the front door Mags gives me a heartfelt hug, wishes me God speed, and asks me to let them know as soon as possible how things work out in Washington. Darcy just turns her back to me and walks into the kitchen. I guess she won't be arranging for the shipping of my golf clubs!

So, off I go again, speeding my way back down the A-1 bound for Newcastle but this time being driven by someone who actually knows what they are doing.

Ray and I have about forty minutes to talk things through on the way down to the airport. He is, not surprisingly, supportive of me. He is a good friend and a pretty smart cookie all things considered. He knows Darcy well and tells me he believes she will come around and find a way to forgive me. He suggests it will just take her some time. I sure hope he is right.

"After all," he adds with more than a hint of sarcasm, "It is not every day that you get your girlfriend handcuffed and locked in the trunk of her car for three hours. Not bad for the first date in eight months. You should give classes."

I can't help but laugh at that and I need a laugh after what has recently transpired. The rest of the ride is spent speculating about my first government sponsored airplane ride, who I will be meeting once I land in D.C., what happens to me and to the document once I turn over the original in Washington, and, that topic exhausted, just where the heck did Archie and Jughead go, and how do we ensure they get held accountable for kidnapping Darcy.

When we pull up at the front of the airport there is a guy in a military uniform of some type standing there. I never can tell which branch is which. He is holding a sign that says 'Mr. Alexander' in bold letters. Ray and I both jump out of the SUV. I wave to the guy, grab my suitcase and backpack, and start to walk over. Just like at the pub a few days ago, Ray grabs me in a big bear hug and tells me to be careful and to let them know what's up as soon as I can.

Lastly he says, "Remember to keep your head down, follow through and hit 'em straight, and don't' worry about Darcy. She loves you and will forgive. She just needs some time."

With Ray expressing the reassurance I desperately needed to hear, I say good-bye and am on my way.

I walk over and present myself to the guy in the uniform. He introduces himself to me quoting some rank or other but I am too flustered, and frankly too tired, to remember his name or his rank. He guides me into the main entrance and then through a rather inconspicuous looking side door and, before I know it, another guy in a uniform has taken over and is walking me directly onto a small but very expensive looking aircraft. I don't know if this guy even introduced himself. Things are moving that quickly on the ground and in my brain.

Almost as soon as I board the plane another person, this time a youngish woman, also in a military uniform, guides me to a seat and says, "Welcome Mr. Alexander. Please take a seat and make yourself comfortable. You might want to fasten your seat belt right away. We are under specific instructions to get underway as soon as we have you on board so we will depart immediately. Apparently there is someone in Washington who wants to speak with you. Our flying time to D.C. will be a little over 7 hours. As luxurious as they are, these jets can really motor when they have to."

She then adds, "Once-air borne either I, or someone else, will come back and see if there is anything that you need."

She departs toward the rear of the plane and I am left all alone in a very comfortable seat on an airplane where there are clearly enough large leather bound seats to accommodate a dozen or more people. The plane soon departs and makes a smooth and uneventful climb to cruising height.

True to her word, the same young woman comes back ten minutes later and asks if I want anything. I ask for a coffee, black with one sugar, and if she might be able to find me something to eat, having had nothing since the night before. The young lady says certainly. She says a coffee will be right up and that someone will make me a sandwich, ham and cheese or turkey and cranberry were the offerings. I opt for a ham and cheese. No prawn flavoured crisps to go with it, darn!

That is pretty much all that I remember before being awakened, almost seven hours later, following a gentle nudge or two to my shoulder.

The same young woman says to me rather sheepishly, "Mr. Alexander, sorry to wake you but we will be landing at Andrews Air Force Base in about fifteen minutes. Please ensure your seat belt is fastened. I hope you enjoyed your flight."

I mumble some type of response but I am not even sure it is intelligible. I then ask her what the local time is. I know it was about 12.45pm by the time we left Newcastle. She replies that it is now 4.50pm local time and reminds me that they are five hours behind U.K time.

I reset my watch and then ask if I have time to use the toilet before landing. She says yes, if I am quick, and then points me in the right direction. While I wander off to the toilet to try and tidy myself up before landing she gingerly removes, from a tray beside my seat, a very cold cup of coffee, and a plate that seems to hold some kind of uneaten sandwich and what we North Americans call potato chips, not crisps.

Once in the toilet (very nice, and very large, by airplane standards I should add) I check myself in the mirror. Looking back at me is a tired looking old man with baggy eyes, mussy hair and a red splotch on one cheek where, I assume, I had rested some part of my anatomy on while asleep for the last nearly seven hours.

I wash my hands and face, use a small disposable toothbrush, and contemplate using the disposable shaving kit but decide against it. One of the benefits of having a beard is you do not have to shave every day. A quick run of damp fingers through my hair will have to pass as a comb.

A swift review of my clothes shows I am relatively tidy, albeit more than just a tad wrinkly. It will have to do and whomever I am to meet will just have to deal with it. No Barbour and Burberry today.

Did I mention I am also incredibly grumpy right now?

Ablutions or what would have to pass for them today done I return to my seat, make sure my seat belt is fastened, and steady myself for what is to come upon landing.

An hour and a half prior to my being woken up by the nice young woman the pilot had made a previously scheduled call to Senator Murchison. Murchison has been named the designated contact for this 'Mission,' having been asked to coordinate my safe and prompt return at the explicit request of the White House.

The pilot advised him that they were about ninety minutes out from Andrews with the passenger safely at hand (and comfortably asleep). The pilot then requested detailed instructions once they land.

Senator Murchison told the pilot that, upon landing, someone from the flight was to escort the passenger directly through a designated exit/entrance at the terminal. There the Senator's aide, in this case a Mr. Ian Ralston, will have a car ready to pick him up and drive him directly to a prearranged meeting site. The pilot was directed to relay these instructions to me once I awoke.

After his call with the flight deck has been completed the Senator again summons Ian Ralston into his office. He outlines to him, "Ian, there is a guy arriving at Andrews in an hour and a half. His name is Jay Alexander and he is the Canadian who brought this entire Lincoln issue to the fore. The Lincoln document has been authenticated by experts in the U.K. and Mr. Alexander is carrying the original document with him. The copy I received by courier is apparently just that, a copy.

"I have arranged for a car to pick Mr. Alexander up at Andrews at 5.00pm. That is the flight's scheduled landing time. I want you to be with the car I send to pick him up. You are to welcome this guy and escort him directly to the White House. The President's Chief of Staff will greet him more formally once you both get there. Your driver has all the instructions for getting Mr. Alexander to the White House and safely through the security gate once there."

Ralston butts in, "So you have decided to go public with this? Do you really think this is wise for your campaign or for the country, Senator?"

"You reticence is noted, Ian. Nothing is decided except that the White House is fully aware of the document and has moved this up to 'priority one' right now. Your job is to get him quickly and comfortably to the meeting.

"Once at the White House, the Chief of Staff, whom I assume you already know, will provide you with any further instructions.

That is assuming he has anything further for you beyond just to say thank-you for your assistance.

"This is an important moment for us and for this country, Ian. Please do what you can to make Mr. Alexander feel welcomed and feel appreciated. He has apparently been through a shit storm of late."

His assignment reluctantly understood Ralston nods to the Senator in agreement and then heads off to the washroom where, using a burner phone, he places another call to Tyrone Thorn. Tyrone answers on the first ring.

"Tyrone, it is Ian. That Canadian guy, Alexander, is arriving at Andrews at 5.00 tonight. He has the original, officially authenticated, Lincoln document with him. Murchison has ordered me to pick him up and take him to the White House. This clearly has been hoisted way up to the top of the White House flag pole."

"Those two fuckin twits, Gunnar and Wyatt, told me they had the document. This Alexander guy must have fleeced them. Dumb fuckers! Wait till I get hold of them. Ian, there is no fucking way you can pick this guy up. Somehow he has to disappear. He cannot deliver this document to the White House."

"Agreed, Tyrone. I know you don't like me to tell you what to do but I have thought this through, so please listen. I will be in a government vehicle with my assigned driver. We will be looking for a military guy bringing Alexander out of a specific entrance at Andrews. I have to assume the guy escorting Alexander won't know who he is or who is picking him up. He will likely just expect someone to pick up the passenger. So you should get to Andrews before 5.00. Go to the exit Murchison told me to go to. Hold up a sign that says something like 'Welcome Mr. Alexander'.

"My bet is the escort will hand him over without any issue at all. Alexander will think all is copacetic and then we will have him, or rather, Tyrone, you will have him!

"I will ask my driver to make a brief stop on the way out to Andrews. This will make sure we are at least 10 minutes late. When

Alexander doesn't walk out I will have my driver as a witness that the guy didn't come out of the building. After an appropriate amount of time, and feigned panic on my part, I can comfortably call Murchison and say Alexander never showed up. That should ruffle more than just a few feathers in the White House, and with Murchison, but will leave me in the clear. It may even succeed in pointing the blame back at Murchison.

"No matter what happens, I am clean and dry. Besides, do you think the White House is going to tell the Canadian Prime Minister that they lost a Canadian citizen at Andrews Airforce Base? No way! The disappearance of Alexander will never become public knowledge. It will never see the light of day. And, Tyrone, I think his disappearance must be permanent. No document, no witness, no fuss. What do you think?"

"Ian, you are right, I don't like being told what to do by you but, I have to admit, this is genius. I will somehow acquire a nice fancy looking black SUV. The Government always uses black SUVs. I will get Billy, you know Billy 'Bones' Beaton, to sit in front and drive all chauffeur-like. I will sit in the back like a White House big shot would. Billy and I will be early. Just make sure you are late. We don't want two vehicles trying to pick this guy up at the same time. Might ring the odd alarm bell!

"Billy Bones, this Alexander guy, and I will take a slight detour out to Arlington. There Alexander will gladly hand over the document once we are finished with him and then he will have to be satisfied with a bullet rather than a free souvenir White House ballpoint pen."

"Perfect, Tyrone. We are agreed. This will work. It has to work! I guess we should get going. You have a vehicle to rent and Billy Bones to recruit. Time is getting tight and I don't want to be late, actually, ha ha, I mean I don't want to be early."

Confident that they finally have this issue under control they both sign off in order to get to work on their parts of the plan.

13

The plane touched down on schedule and I am courteously, but hurriedly, hustled off the plane, led through a series of doors, and end up out the front of what I assume to be some type of terminal. There is a man standing there holding a sign that says 'Welcome Home Mr. Alexander.' While I am glad to touch down, I am actually still a very long way from home but, given recent events, why quibble?

My military escort is the pleasant young woman from my flight. She quickly points out to me the gentleman with the sign. She hands me my suitcase which she has carried despite my incessant protestations. I have 3 older sisters and they drilled into me that men don't let women carry their suitcases.

My escort then offers me a quick salute (not sure why) and leaves me to find my own way over to an awaiting vehicle.

The guy holding the sign is dressed in a rather ill-fitting black suit and a white shirt that could use a visit to the laundry. He is a tall, gangly looking, fellow with rather unkempt hair. White socks are visible as his trousers don't quite reach the top of his shoes. Not what one would expect from the driver sent by a senior Government official. I guess austerity is everywhere these days and good help, or good clothes, hard to find. Don't they sell Burberry in the USA?

Mr. String Bean opens the back door of the vehicle for me and I climb in while he walks around and places my suitcase in the trunk. I shouldn't be so judgemental but this guy certainly doesn't look the part according to my preconceptions about White House protocol and class. Maybe my imagination has taken flight again?

There is a man already seated in the back. He is dressed in a marginally nicer suit than the driver. At least his shirt is presentable and he is sporting a decent tie. He extends his hand out for me to shake and says, "Hello Mr. Alexander and welcome to D.C. My name is Ian Ralston. I trust you had a nice flight. These new business and government jets are quite something aren't they?"

He adds, "I am the Communication Director for Senator Jefferson Murchison. I have been asked to personally see that you get to a meeting with Senior White House officials as soon as I can. We were originally to attend the meeting at the White House proper but, due to potential press leaks, the meeting has been moved to a still safe, but much more clandestine, location in Arlington, Virginia. Have you ever been to D.C. or to Arlington, Mr. Alexander?"

I mumble something quite unimaginative in return about not knowing much about Virginia or D.C.

Whenever I get nervous I tend to fill in every moment of silence with comments or questions. Sometimes this borders on babbling. The more nervous I am, the more incoherent my babbling becomes. Given that I am about to meet some unnamed White House dignitary, or two or three, and likely a famous Senator, I am certainly nervous. So, sadly for my well-kept public imagine, I let the questions and blathering spill out.

I ask Ian Ralston, "How long before we get to the meeting?"

"About forty minutes."

"Who will be there?" I ask next.

"I am afraid I don't know for sure—likely Senator Murchison and one or two Senior White House officials, among others perhaps."

Trying to keep the conversation going I add, "So you work with Senator Murchison. What is he like?"

"Smart and dedicated."

This is getting painful, "How long have you worked in Washington?"

"Six years."

The conversation goes on just like this for over forty minutes, me asking questions that become more inane as the trip progresses and this Ralston guy responding with the minimum number of words required. The less he says, the more nervous I become and the more idiotic, almost desperate, my questions and comments become.

I must admit that when I think of a Communications Director for a Senior US Senator I would expect someone gregarious, warm, informative, and, above all, a good to excellent communicator. Ian Ralston does not live up to my expectations in any way. Who knows what he expected of me?

I wouldn't even say that Ralston was overly polite. Brusque or sullen might be the best words to describe him. As a result, the drive to Arlington seems to take forever.

After what is an excruciatingly painful (from my perspective anyway) drive out to Arlington we finally arrive at a rather unimpressive looking rancher in the middle of a sub-division. This hardly looks like the place Senior White House people and Senators would meet. But all this hush-hush about a clandestine location has my 'Spidey Sense' in sleep mode.

Once inside the front door of the rancher, things change rapidly. The man who introduced himself as Ian Ralston immediately slams me into a wall, throws me to the floor, gives me a couple of quick kicks to the ribs, while snarling at me, "You think you're clever, asshole? Let's see how clever you really are. You have something we want and you are not going to leave here until we have it. In fact you might not be leaving here anyway."

He then pulls out a hand gun that has an extra-long barrel and points it at me rather threateningly. He demonstrates complete confidence with how he handles the revolver. He is clearly familiar with fire arms. It takes me a few seconds to realize the hand gun is extra-long because it has a silencer on the end.

With that realization still playing in my head, the front door opens and the string bean driver strides in carrying my suitcase, looks down and spits on me. He adds a few more kicks, grins and says, "welcome to the last day of your life, asshole."

This Ralston guy says, "Not so fast, Bones. You will get your turn. Help me get this guy down the stairs to the basement. Then we can have a good root around his suitcase and a good root around anyplace else we have to look."

I try my best to resist but the impact from the tumble to the floor, the rib kicks, and the fact there are two of them, has me at a big disadvantage. These two are both strong and determined and one of them has a gun pointed at me. They literally drag me down about 10 stairs into a rather stark looking room at the bottom. There they throw me onto the floor again, followed by a few more kicks.

The room we are in has a basic concrete floor with a work bench in one corner, a weigh bench in another, and a simple set of shelves against one wall. All the walls are painted dullish white and the ceiling is unfinished, just open joists.

Before I can gather my wits this Bones guy fastens my hands behind my back with some type of plastic zip-tie thingy.

They ask me for the keys to my suitcase and, as I refuse, I get a few more kicks and slaps as they roughly fish through my pockets until they drag out the key.

Once unlocked, they dump the suitcase upside down on the floor and start to rifle through it like a couple of crazed grave diggers. They look and look, tearing out the lining and even ripping the handles off my case. They don't find what they are looking for. "Where is it, asshole," the Bones guy says. Where is the f'ing document?"

"I gave it to your bullet headed buddies back in the U.K.," I manage to squeak out, hoping to talk my way out of this mess by using false bravado.

"Bull shit," this Ralston guy says. "We know that was a fake that you gave those two goofs." Then he adds, "Ian told me you had it with you on the plane and Senator Murchison told him you did as well, so we know you have it. Where the fuck is it?"

"I guess I left it on the plane then." I get another kick for that.

In the midst of my panic I wonder to myself, if this just guy said, "Ian told me you had it with you on the plane," who is this guy holding a gun to my head if not Ian Ralston?

Not finding the document, and now clearly perplexed, they both sit down for a minute or two evidently trying to understand what is going on. Sadly for me, they are still pointing the pistol my way. Bones looks at this Ralston guy and says, "What the fuck are we missing, Tyrone?"

Now I am even more confused. This guy is obviously not Ian Ralston. He must be that Tyrone Thorn guy that Andy's ex-FBI friend flagged, the head honcho of the so called Brotherhood. As I roll this around in my mind it doesn't bring any comfort. Andy's words about "ex-military and dangerous" just add to my alarm.

After what seems like an endless time (fear does that to you) this Bones guy excitedly shouts out, "His backpack, Tyrone. He had a backpack when he came out to the car at the airport. It must still be in the car. That must be where the document is," and, after a pleased look of acknowledgment from Tyrone, he rushes out to retrieve my backpack from the vehicle.

To make sure I stay still and behave myself this Ralston/Tyrone guy approaches me and, standing just two feet away, points the gun squarely at the middle of my forehead and taunts me by saying, "Not going to try anything foolish are you, my Canadian friend?"

Holy shit, I think to myself. What am I going to do? Is this it for me? Once they find the document in my backpack does this guy pull the trigger?"

Then it dawns on me even more clearly that, once they get the document from my backpack, I am not leaving here alive. My thoughts immediately turn to my kids, my grandkids, to Darcy, and perhaps strangely, to who will look after Jack, my dog.

At about 5.10pm Ian Ralston and his driver arrive at the Airport. They wait for a few minutes with the driver standing outside holding up a 'Welcome Mr. Alexander' sign. Ian Ralston makes it a point to come out of the car several times and say quite loudly to the driver things like, "Where is that guy? He is supposed to be here. What's keeping him? The Senator said he would be here."

After a few more minutes he tells the driver to go inside and ask around to find out where this Mr. Alexander is or where he has gone.

As he enters the main building the driver almost immediately sees a couple of men in Air Force uniforms. He walks up to them and asks if anyone knows anything about an arriving civilian passenger named Jay Alexander. Adding, "We are here to pick him up."

One of the two says, "Are you kidding me? A black SUV picked that guy up ten minutes ago. What the hell is going on with you guys anyway? No offense but you people need to get your schedules straight."

The driver sprints back out to the car and tells Ralston that this Alexander guy was already picked up.

Sticking to his clever plan, Ralston feigns panic and hurriedly calls the Senator on his cell. When the Senator picks up Ralston dramatically says, "Senator, it's me, Ian. What is going on? Apparently your Mr. Alexander was picked up about fifteen minutes ago in a black government vehicle. Did you send two cars? Did you change the plan? I am confused."

The Senator is stunned. After a further brief exchange the Senator barks, "You stay there until I say otherwise. Maybe there is some kind of mix-up and whoever picked him up will bring him back. In the meantime I am going to get to the bottom of this with the White House. Call me the minute you learn anything." He closes off with, "Shit, shit, shit."

In a state of alarm and confusion, the Senator reaches for his office phone to call his White House contact. But before he starts the call his phone rings. Thinking it is Ralston he snatches the phone up right away and says. "Ian, what have you got?"

To his surprise it is not Ian Ralston but his friend, Andy Hutchins.

"Jefferson, it is me, Andy, we need to talk."

"Andy, sorry I don't have time right now. Things have gone sideways with your friend Alexander and I am up to my ass in crocodile feces."

"Jefferson, this is about Jay Alexander and it is critically important. Please give me three minutes. I have just learned something you need to hear. Please!"

"Okay, Andy, you got exactly three minutes, not a second more."

"Jefferson, you remember I told you I was having my ex-FBI buddy try and chase down those two guys who were following Jay all over England. Well he, Duncan, promised to send me a photo so I could get Jay to make a positive identification that we had the right two guys."

"Yes, so what? We were pretty sure we knew that already. Tick tock, Andy, tick tock."

"I am getting to it. I just got the photo from Duncan via an e-mail attachment. The photo shows four guys in heavy camo and armed to the teeth standing front and centre in one of those 'free the land' protests in Idaho. If you recall it was the protest that turned so violent several years ago. According to the photo caption all four are reputed to be active and proud members of the Brothers of Freedom.

"Two of the guys in the photo are the two assholes who have been harassing Jay, Gunnar Nielsen and Wyatt Bing. Of the other two in the photo, one is a guy named Tyrone Thorn, alleged to be the D.C.-based head of the Brothers of Freedom. You are not going to believe who the 4th guy is. Jefferson, the 4th guy is none other than Tyrone Thorn's step brother, Ian Ralston; the same guy you hired as your Communications Director, the same guy I met at your dinner party, the same guy who was so wishy-washy defending you at the Press Conference. He's the leak, Jefferson. He's the leak. Ian Ralston is the God damned leak."

"Fuck me! Worse than that, Andy, I sent him to pick up your friend Alexander at the Airport. Ralston just called to say Alexander never showed up. It now seems certain that these Brothers of Freedom have snatched Alexander to get at the Lincoln document and that son-of-a-bitch Ralston orchestrated it. I need to go now Andy. I need to get on this ASAP."

"Quickly, one last thing, Jefferson. According to my friend, Duncan, this Tyrone character runs this Brotherhood out of a safe house in Arlington, Virginia. Duncan says the FBI apparently has him under close and near constant surveillance. That is where I would start if I had to find Jay. And, Jefferson, don't let anything happen to Jay. As friends go he is aces, a wonderful guy, and has put his ass on the line for you. Now go get him Jefferson!"

It doesn't take too long for the Senator to get things moving quickly. He just has to make one phone call to the White House and things fly into action.

Never mind propriety and the right thing to do, never mind the document, if things go south with this kidnapping the White House would have a major crisis on their hands. How do you explain losing a Canadian from right off a U.S. Airforce Base? Murchison would be in even more trouble having his Communications Director identified as being complicit in the disappearance. And, Senator Murchison, can just hear the reporters ask, "How does a known relative of the leader of the Brothers of Freedom get a senior job in a Senator's office? What happened to due diligence when reference checking Senator? Who else have you got working in your office Senator, Al Qaeda? Hamas? The Taliban?"

Try and explain or answer those questions and the myriad of others that would hound the Senator for years and, most certainly, end his White House aspirations for good!

So, not surprisingly, things move very quickly in the White House when diplomacy, careers, and reputations are in danger. Very, very quickly! The first law of politics demonstrated in living colour, 'above all else, cover your ass.'

As Billy Bones sprints out to the car to retrieve the backpack he notices another black SUV parked right behind his. He knows it wasn't there earlier. As he stops to try and figure out what's what, the front passenger door of the SUV opens and out steps a guy wearing one of those famous FBI windbreakers. His partner, similarly attired, steps out of the driver's side of the SUV at virtually the same time.

The FBI Agent closest to the curb says, "Well, well, if it isn't Billy 'Bones' Beaton. Fancy seeing you in front of the house of the Hitler Youth movement. Going somewhere in such a hurry, Billy?"

"You ain't got nothin' on me, so stop all the hassling. I am just dropping something off for Tyrone and heading back home for my supper."

"Why the sprint then, Billy, and why leave the front door open? That makes us suspicious. What did you just drop off? Or rather, who did you just drop off? It wasn't a Canadian by the name of Jay Alexander was it? I think maybe we should have a look inside."

"You can't go in there without a warrant."

"Did you hear that partner? Billy just said go ahead on in. He says Tyrone won't mind if we go in and say hello. Thanks for being so understanding, Billy."

Thinking more clearly about illegal search and seizure, the Agent continues, "Besides, this is a crime-riddled neighbourhood, isn't it partner? We see a guy running out the front door of a house and heading to his car, the guy a known felon no less, leaving the door wide open as he flees. I think we have a crime in progress here. We better go inside and make sure everything is okay. Somebody might be hurt in there."

That said he winks at his partner. While keeping an eye on Billie Bones, they wait for about a minute for a second black SUV to pull up. When the second vehicle arrives two more FBI Agents leap out of it. The Agent who is clearly in charge points at one of the two new arrivals and says, "Boynton, you stay here with Billy Bones." He then points at the other new arrival and instructs, "You, Jenkin, get moving. Come with us. The three of us are going into the house and see what or who Thorn is hiding in there. Stay vigilant as this Tyrone Thorn is not to be taken lightly. The guy is ex-military. He is probably armed and he knows how to use a gun."

In a flurry of motion, revolvers drawn, the three of them race up the sidewalk and enter the house.

Down in the basement, Tyrone is taunting me as he holds the pistol which is still pointed directly at my head.

He says, "I don't get you Alexander. We have enough panty waist liberals in this country. Why the hell do we need a commie Canadian sticking his nose in where it doesn't belong? Even when you get a clear message from my friends that we don't want or need your interference you still persist. You are one stubborn fucker and one dumb one too."

He continues, "I suppose it won't matter in the long run. Your time is just about up and so is your little adventure with this Lincoln paper thing. Once my little buddy, Billy Bones, returns with the backpack we will put an end to this charade. Then you can kiss your Canadian ass, and the rest of your worthless life, good fuckin' bye, courtesy of a bullet right between your commie Canadian eyes. I look forward to finally pulling the trigger myself."

Continuing to have the pistol pointed at my head he goes over to one of the shelves and drags out what looks like a large plastic drop cloth. Now I am certain my time is up. No way to talk my way out of this. I am not sure how I feel... just numb I guess.

Hearing a noise behind him, and through a self-satisfied smirk, Tyrone says, "Bring it over here, Billy. Let's have a look inside that bag and finish this thing once and for all."

But the voice that answers isn't Billy's. Instead Tyrone hears, "Yes, Tyrone, I think it is probably a real good time to finish this thing. Now drop the gun, step away from Mr. Alexander, put your hands up over your head, and get down on your knees. And don't try anything stupid. Oh, and one more thing, get ready to say goodbye to the famous four freedoms you and your Brethren have been so up in arms about. Where you are going this basement is going to look pretty fucking good and real freedoms pretty fucking rare!"

A stunned Tyrone Thorn immediately drops the gun, puts his hands behind his head and kneels down. It looks like he has done this before. He shows virtually no emotion as his hands are quickly pulled down behind his back and cuffs roughly slapped on. He seems to be resigned to what is coming and so makes no effort in responding either verbally or physically. I guess he figures his buddy Conrad can fix this or he is smart enough to realize his goose is really and truly cooked and, hence, no sense trying to fight it.

After a few exchanges of "are you all right Mr. Alexander," the restraints being removed from my wrists, my garbled expressions of gratitude, a few cursory quick pokes to see if I am injured, and a major drop in my blood pressure about the only thing I can say is, "I think I might need to change my pants."

With that, all three Agents laugh and the one in charge says, through a barely contained chuckle, "Let's get you some clean pants, get you checked out for any serious injuries, and find you a place to relax and catch your breath. I understand there is someone very important who wants to talk to you."

As we walk out the front door of Tyrone's house I am nearly blinded by the lights of at least a dozen police vehicles. There is also an ambulance amongst the array of police cruisers. I guess it is there just in case things went south. Hopefully it is not there for me. At least there is no hearse amongst this array.

I see a couple of guys, presumably Tyrone and his pal Bones, each being pushed into the back of separate vehicles. One of the 'would be' prisoners enters easily, steely and calmly, ducking his head as he slides in. The other seems to be a flaying mass of arms and legs and protestations. Both these vehicles then quickly depart with prisoners safely in hand.

A paramedic comes over from the ambulance to see me. He has a cursory look at me, pats me here and there, asks me a few questions, and them proclaims, "Looks like you will be just fine, Mr. Alexander. A few bruises but nothing serious. You can get on your way. No need to ride in the back of this 'bus' with us tonight." He gives a brief nod to the Agent in charge and walks off.

The next thing I am aware of I am in the back seat of a black SUV being driven by one of my rescuers. The fellow in the passenger seat has introduced both himself and his partner but I am too stupefied to take in any names. I've never been good with remembering names anyway. This time I have a good excuse.

After a few minutes of us driving, I assume heading into Washington proper, the Agent in the passenger seat hands me a phone and says, "Someone wants to talk to you."

Taking the phone I manage to get out a weak "hello" when the voice on the other end identifies himself as Senator Jefferson Murchison.

"Mr. Alexander, Jay, can I call you Jay? You have had a hell of a day. Lots of stories to tell your grandkids which, I am hoping, I can persuade you not to do. That we will get into later. In the meantime we need to make sure we take the very best care of you. We really have not done a very good job of that up until now. And, by the way, your good friend, Andy, says hi!

"We had already booked a suite for you at the Watergate Hotel in town. The Agents will take you there straight away and get you checked in. This will provide you with some well-deserved time to unwind and reflect on what must have been a nightmare. The White House was hoping to talk to you this evening but, given all that you have been through, we will reschedule and have you come over tomorrow morning. I hope that is alright with you?"

Without pausing to think things through I reply, "Senator, thank you for your kind words and for your consideration. Truth is, as tired and beat up as I am I'm also quite a bit pissed off and very much on edge. I just want to get this entire episode behind me as soon as I can and get back safely and quickly to my home in Canada. If the offer is still on can we do this tonight? I am willing if you are."

"Wonderful! Perfect! If you are certain you are feeling up to it we will get that done. I will have the Agents take you to the Hotel now. You can rest for a bit, shower and change, and then the Agents will take you to the White House to meet with us there."

Before I can say change into what, the Senator adds, "We will arrange to deliver a fresh change of clothes for you. No need to worry about anything. The two Agents with you right now will not let you out of their sight until you are safely at the White House. Well that is not quite true," he adds with a small laugh. "They will leave you alone in your room but they will be right outside in the corridor. Try not to get into any more trouble," he then says, as he tries to insert some more levity.

"It is just after seven o'clock now. Do you think you would be up for a meeting at the White House at ten tonight?"

I reply in the affirmative. I had almost seven hours sleep on the plane and have enough adrenaline pumping through me to keep me awake for a month.

The call over and a meeting agreed to, the Agents and I continue on our journey to the hotel. Oddly, my nervous blathering on the drive out to Arlington has turned to a very quiet bout of introspection. I would suggest that 'vacant' and 'spent' are the best words to describe how I feel just now. The rest of the trip to the hotel is completed in silence. I can only assume the Agents know how I feel so they leave me alone to get lost in my own world of quiet contemplation.

After arrival at the hotel, and a seamless check-in, my two shadows accompany me up to my room. There I find a complete set of new clothes waiting for me. A pair of Ferragamo loafers, a Harris Tweed jacket from Brooks Brothers, some Italian slacks of a brand I am unfamiliar with, and a white oxford cloth long sleeve button down shirt. How they figured all this out in such a hurry and got the sizes correct I am not sure. Andy again?

Whoever did this also included new socks and underwear plus a nice silk tie, Burberry no less. However they forgot a belt. I guess I will need to wear the one I have on. Luckily the color will match my new Italian slacks. One should not look out of fashion when visiting the White House I am told. I guess someone should have told Billy Bones that.

After a lie down of about an hour and a half, followed by a shave and a shower, I feel better. But no sooner have I manage to guzzle down a quick club house sandwich and beer, ordered from room service, than there is a knock on the door telling me it is time to go. So, off I go again, me in the back of the same black SUV, for the ten-minute drive to whatever and whoever awaits me at the White House.

14

I wouldn't know the inside of the White House from a brothel, not that I have ever been inside either. But I know what the White House looks like from the outside and we are definitely here, the White House that is, not a brothel.

After a brief stop we are officially cleared through the main gate. Car parked, we go through a side entrance to the 'House' itself. There I am greeted by Senator Murchison and another gentleman who looks vaguely familiar. Murchison greets me warmly, almost like we are old friends. This other gentleman, his actions more business mannered, introduces himself as Wilson Finlayson. I immediately recognize the name as one frequently in the news. Finlayson is the President's Chief of Staff. Apparently he is the contact that got the FBI to my rescue so quickly. Despite my difficulty with names his name I will remember.

The Senator and Finlayson escort me up a set of stairs, down a couple of corridors, and then into a large, tastefully appointed, but surprisingly comfortable looking room. There is a casually dressed gentleman standing there, his back to me, his hands folded behind his back. He is facing an open fire. When he turns to greet us I am immediately floored, and the floor is the last place I want to be after my recent visit to Tyrone's house.

Coming over to greet me, with his hand warmly extended, is none other than the President of the United States. He is tall, slim, and looks exceedingly fit. He is, as one would expect, immaculately groomed. He has perfectly styled grey hair, cut fashionably short. He has the most intense, almost piercing, steel blue eyes I have ever seen. He is wearing a brown cashmere sweater and, believe it or not, blue jeans, Wranglers I think. 'Only the W is silent.' Like Murchison did, he greets me very warmly with a firm, yet friendly handshake.

With an engaging, yet slightly bemused, smile he says, "Mr. Alexander, you have been a very busy man. It is my pleasure to meet you. I am so glad that you are well and this ordeal you have gotten yourself caught up in seems to be finally coming to an end." He then adds, a bit pensively, "Well at least for you."

"Mr. President," I manage somehow to stammer out over a knotted tongue, "The pleasure is all mine, I assure you. I am honoured. Never in my life did I think I would be in such esteemed company as I am at this moment."

"Don't flatter me, Mr. Alexander, or may I call you Jay? You may learn that I am not all that esteemed or all that great company." He smiles again. "And, for the next while, you need not call me Mr. President. I think just my name, Charles, will suffice. No need for formalities in this room."

Introductions and niceties dealt with, the President surprises everyone in the room by saying to the Senator and to the Chief of Staff, "That will be all gentlemen. If I need one of you I will have someone track you down. Don't go too far just in case. Jay and I have several important things to discuss."

With a wave of his hand he dismisses the other two and motions me to one of two vacant chairs beside the fire. He asks if I would like a drink, and then adds, "I understand Scotch whisky is your preference." Without waiting for my response, he retrieves a carafe from a nearby side table and pours two fingers of whisky into an exquisite crystal glass, which he then hands to me.

"Neat, I presume he says," again without waiting for an answerer as he pours one for himself.

He walks back over toward the fire and takes the other chair. He raises his glass to me and says "slainte mhath." We then begin a conversation that will stay with me forever.

"Jay, again I am so sorry about what you have had to endure over the last several days. I have been well briefed and can appreciate just how difficult this must have been, both physically and emotionally."

Yes, I think to myself and that doesn't even speak to my losing Darcy again.

"To begin, I have to ask, out of curiosity, why not just surrender the Lincoln document to your pursuers? You are Canadian. Issues regarding my country's oft disappointing and too often buried past should not be of concern for you. Hell, they seldom seem of a concern to enough Americans these days. Why the resilience and the stick-to-it-iveness? Why see this out all the way to the end? Especially in the face of threats and violence."

Before I can reply, he says, "Oh and by the way do you have the document with you?"

I remove the document from my backpack, so much for White House security, and gently hand it to him. He gives it a cursory look and places it on the side table, next to carafe of whisky. It is clear he has already seen a copy, likely via the Senator, and is very familiar with the contents.

"So why do all this, Jay," he repeats?

"I suppose the easy answer to that, Mr. President, I mean Charles," I add awkwardly, "Is that it seemed the right thing to do. And once the ball got rolling the task just seemed to be more important and my stubbornness more pronounced."

I have to admit calling the President by his first name does not come without some unease.

"I think that speaks volumes about your character, Jay. So, you have obviously read the document. What do you think about it?"

"Well Sir, (I just cannot get round to the Charles part) I doubt it is really my opinion you want on this."

"On the contrary, Jay, your opinion is precisely what I want to hear."

"If you insist, Sir," (no Charles again this time). "I think what is in this document poses an enormous challenge. I am a bit of a Lincoln buff, old university courses and many books read on the man and the era. No one really knows what he might have been able to accomplish had he lived out his second, and perhaps even third or fourth terms.

"I think the document demonstrates that he cared deeply about all Americans, both northerner and southerner and both white and black. I believe he clearly saw the need for reconciliation and for restitution. However, the cost in land and money in1865 is a long way away from the cost today. And this doesn't even begin to address the land transfer side of the equation. This document, Mr. President, presents what you call an immense dilemma and I am glad it is you, and not me, who has to decide what to do with it."

I add to his question by posing a number of questions and comments of my own.

I offer, "I suspect you have a lot to consider Mr. President, I mean Charles. Is it legal? If yes, is it enforceable? Who would be in favour? I guess that is obvious. But who would be lined up against it and how seriously would they object? How much would it cost? How big would the blow back be? How would it benefit your country? What damage would it do to your country? Is your country ready for this at this point in time? What about your legacy? Would it be enhanced or severely damaged?"

Continuing on, "While it is not any of my business as an outsider, I would suggest your country is in a bit of a mess right now. The divisions within seem to be both hardening and widening. In my less than expert opinion things appear to have become very polarized down here."

"Quite a comprehensive understanding of the challenges I face, Jay. So what would you do if you were me?"

"Ha, ha, nice try, Sir! I have enough problems of my own. No way would I want anything to do with making the decisions surrounding this document. That is squarely in your bailiwick. As for the polarization in your country, that is perhaps even tougher."

"And what might you do about that, Jay," he asks somewhat rhetorically.

I am not sure he really wants me to answer but I actually relish the opportunity. I am undeterred.

"You know, Sir, actually, how would you know? But I have some knowledge and experience in the area of managing change and transition, both of the organizational and personal nature. I think, in an overly simplistic way, that you have a huge change management problem down here stateside. And, I think it is something you, in America, and we, in Canada, currently share with most other Western democracies."

"How so, Jay, please go on. I am truly interested. I would like to hear more. Please continue."

"Well the hard truth about change is that people actually don't like it very much, especially when they feel they have no control over it.

"You see every change brings with it a loss of some kind. When we move to something new, even if it is something we really crave, we always leave something behind. We have to give something up, intended or not, tangible or not. Even more damaging is we often don't realize what we have lost until it is gone.

"The tangible side, the physical aspects of a change, is one thing and it is usually impactful. The personal or psychological side however is the real issue. How do we feel about what we have to give up in order to move forward? How do we feel about what we have lost or are about to lose? Will we be better off or worse off?

"Whenever our comfort zone is invaded we feel uneasy and anxious. We often knee jerk react right away or sometime later after we fully understand or feel the impacts. Our reactions are often unpredictable and emotionally based.

"The world these days is moving at a rapid pace. But it is not just technology that is driving change. More impactful, on the personal level, are social, economic, and cultural changes, and there are many, many of these.

"People look around today and they don't see what they used to see or what they have always taken for granted. Social mores are different; the type of work people do now is different; the jobs millions of people used to do are gone. The LGBTQ movement is changing how we define sexuality or how we define gender. Climate change has laid out a huge challenge, attracting both believers and non-believers, with fanatics on both sides. For the first time in history we actually have five generations trying to express their unique cultural norms all at the same time, too often not understanding each other or not trusting each other. Immigration is at an all-time high. Illegal immigration also seems to be at an all-time high, brought on by war, hunger or desperation. While people can sympathize with those camped on your country's border it seems, to me at least, they have a harder time showing empathy.

"Hell, whoops, excuse my language, but, according to my parents, back in the 60's you could get beaten up just for wearing bell bottoms or having long hair. Traditional society didn't accept these simple changes in appearance. Something as simple as HAIR was a major societal point of dispute. You have to concede that hair is a pretty minor societal difference compared to what we see today.

"Today people are feeling overwhelmed. They cannot always cope. Even if they can, they may not like what they see around them. They need time to debate, time to adjust, and time to accept.

"Experts say most people deal with change in a similar fashion to the way they deal with grief. It is often viewed that the first two stages of both are denial and resistance. People will ignore what is going on around them, denying that it is real or denying it will have any impact on them. Once they begin to realize it is real, and it impacts them, resistance or push back can emerge. Given the opportunity, people will revert to the prior conditions as soon as possible, rejecting the pressures society is placing on them to move forward or disputing the compelling reasons to move forward. They just hope it will all go away. They either bury their heads in the sand or come out swinging. Their old 'comfort zone' looks pretty good to them.

"Purposely or accidentally, along come politicians who promise to bring back the good old days. These politicians allow or implore people to reject the pressures and requirements to move forward. People find, or are handed, someone to blame and then they are encouraged to hammer away at the change masters thus creating 'a common enemy.'

"Next thing you know, large numbers of people are up in arms about what is changing; the new faces, the new culture, the new social mores. It is the fault of immigrants. It is the black lives matter movement that is to blame. It is the LGBTQ movement. It is the 'Woke' folks that are to blame. It is the President and his damn 'Lincoln document' and his pandering to the distant past.

"People are easily led (or rather mislead) to believe, often with the help of various social media, that if all this went away all would be fine!

"Of course nothing could be further from the truth. For example, again in my humble opinion, one of the driving forces of Brexit was an emotional response to immigration. Anyone who travelled in the U.K., and I have travelled there extensively, would have known that without people from Eastern Europe working in the U.K. the entire economy would collapse from a lack of available labour force. These so called interlopers weren't taking jobs. They were filling the jobs that were/are necessary to fill for life to go on. But these 'new faces' became the convenient common enemy for those feeling disenfranchised or unfulfilled. Unscrupulous or uninformed Leaders leapt at the chance to use this as an avenue to gain power or achieve a very personal agenda. Emotion prevailed over logic.

"This change management notion I am pedaling is an over simplification, I know, but I think it is worth considering. The thing to understand about change is that people will get there eventually given enough information, given enough encouragement, given enough support and given enough time. They won't get there by hearing false promises that we can all go back to the way things were and it will all be fine.

"People need to remember that the 'good old days' were not always so shit hot... sorry again, so darn hot I mean. The 'good old days' just look more comfortable and wonderful in the rear view mirror.

"The trick is we need to help people along while things are changing. This might require getting the high flyers, the early adapters, and the zealots to slow down. Positive progress needs society to reach back and lend a hand and help those who are having trouble catching up or struggling to understanding why things are changing. Governments and Leaders everywhere need to communicate and care and to effectively communicate 'that they care'. Continue the positive move forward, fine, but make sure you help people move along with you at a pace they can cope with.

"I am in no way saying things are moving in the wrong direction. I am likely as far to the left as your Senator Murchison is purported to be. But the Left, demanding what they do as fervently as they do, doesn't help either. The Left needs to be patient too. This might encourage the Right to be a little less reactionary and angry.

"I do not believe for one second that people are naturally bigoted, mean or uncaring. Quite the opposite! People care. But you tell people often enough that they are being taken advantage of, being forced to move in the wrong direction, or they are going to lose everything because of some 'invented common enemy' and they will react negatively. They will get angry. They will dig their heels in. They will resist.

"Sadly, people can be, and are being manipulated by folks who seek power over propriety, decency, and truth because it suits their agenda or fulfils their lust for power.

"That Mr. President... Sir... er Charles... is my two bits worth, for what it is worth, if anything. Not much else I can say except it has been a pleasure talking with you. Oh, and I do think that Lincoln's promise needs some type of response even if it is just an acknowledgment of wrong doing and an apology to the ancestors of the millions who had their lives ruled and ruined by slavery."

"For not much, Jay, that is a hell of a lot of two bits. You are quite a long winded SOB aren't you, and I am not apologizing for my language," he adds with a chuckle.

He continues, "I seldom get to talk to someone one-on-one who doesn't come to me with a specific agenda or requiring some type of quid pro quo arrangement. It is refreshing to just hear from someone who doesn't have an ulterior motive."

"Well, Sir, maybe you should try and arrange it so that you can do this more often. Get out of this building and find a way to talk to real people; not the politicians, the lobbyists and the grandstanders. Maybe try listening and learning by walking around and talking to people of all walks of life. Easier said than done I am sure. But if anyone can do it I am sure it is you.

"Can I ask you one question, Sir?"

"Of course, Jay, what is it you want to ask? Go ahead, fire away."

"Well, Sir, if I can be so bold, what are you going to do about the Lincoln document?"

"You don't mess around do you, Jay?

"The truth is, Jay, I am not 100% sure what I am going to do at this point. It seems to be a lose-lose proposition. The impact of applying the Lincoln promise in today's America may not be possible given the economic and social costs and given that 150 plus years have dramatically changed the make-up and infrastructure of the former 'Secessionist States'. Money is one thing. And the economic costs would be prohibitive. But taking homes and land away from people who have been there for 150 years to give it to someone else, well, how does one do that and not cause chaos and hatred.

"This would likely end up in the courts and would lead to a series of court battles that may take years and end up leaving vast numbers of people unsatisfied, angry and, even broken.

"Something must be done about the Lincoln promise, but a full and complete implementation of this document, of that I am much less sure.

"I hope that is not too evasive, Jay, but to be totally honest that is about all I can tell you right now.

"Leadership often brings with it very challenging decisions for which there is never one right answer and, sometimes, there are only bad answers. But I guess that comes with the territory and, as Harry Truman was known to say, 'The Buck Stops Here.'"

All I can do, in response to the President's frank and honest response to my question, is to provide a knowing smile and leave it at that. The meeting is clearly over and all that remains is to say thank you, wish the President good luck with his dilemma, and exit stage right (or is it to be exit stage 'Left').

After exchanging a few more kind words, a warm handshake, and a sincere thank-you, I leave feeling both relieved and inspired. I am carrying with me, in my backpack, three White House pen and pencil sets, one for me and one for each of my children, and a White House tie pin to go with my new Burberry tie. I didn't get offered a gift for my dog Jack.

As I walk away, and the door closes behind me, I am pretty sure, but will never be 100% certain, that I can hear the sound of a paper shredder emanating from the room I just left the President alone in. But, then again, you know me and my over active imagination.

The President's Assistant, who is seated outside this room, provides me with my instructions for my return home tomorrow. I then say good night to Senator Murchison and Chief of Staff Finlayson. They were both hovering near the door, anxious I am sure, to grill the President on what has just transpired. They none-the-less kindly thank me for my efforts and wish me a safe and swift return home. Senator Murchison even goes as far as to suggest he will keep in touch.

After I am walked back along the corridors and down the staircase, another black SUV returns me to the hotel. On the way I am informed that a government jet will take me directly back to Victoria in the morning. The scheduled departure is 7.15am. A car is to pick me up at the hotel at 6.30am. To say I am happy to be heading home would be an understatement.

Once back at the hotel I enjoy a small, mini bar assisted, night cap and try and sleep despite the events of last ten or eleven days bouncing around in my brain.

My last thoughts, before finally drifting off to sleep, are of the kids, of the grandkids, of Darcy, and of Jack, my dog. I also know I can finally sleep comfortably seeing that there are two FBI Agents in the corridor right outside my room.

15

Day Thirteen

I get up at the ungodly hour, at least for me, of 6.00am. I quickly shower, complete my other ablutions, dress, and head out the door. There are two new, new to me at least, FBI Agents in the corridor. They respectfully introduce themselves to me and, in keeping with my usual pattern of not paying enough attention when meeting people for the first time, I immediately forget their names. Somewhere in my past I was taught to ensure a firm handshake and good eye contact when meeting someone for the first time. I have this skill down pat, so much so that the name never registers with my brain when it is given.

The Agent who appears to be in charge reconfirms that my flight is scheduled to depart at 7.15am. He further confirms that, as I am slated to be the only passenger, the plane is not going anywhere without me, so we do not really need to rush. This gives me an idea, one that just dawns on me at this very instant.

I ask if we can make one quick stop on the way to the airport, even if it means a slight detour. The senior Agent essential tells me that 'my wish is their command.' He adds that they have both been instructed to take the very best care of me. It is always nice to feel special.

When I tell them where I want to stop they don't really express surprise. I am not sure how much the two Agents know about my recent experience but they seem to understand why this stop would be important to me. The stop I ask to make is at the Lincoln Memorial. I feel an overwhelming need to go there and pay my respects.

We leave the hotel and drive to the Memorial, parking as close as we can. Once there I spend a few moments of quiet reflection, thinking back on my recent experiences and contemplating the challenges that Lincoln must have faced in his tragically short, but ever so remarkable, life. As it is quite early in the morning I have much of the area around the 'Memorial' to myself. This makes the visit all that much more special.

This important stop made, we get to Andrews Air Force a bit later than originally planned. I say good bye to my two escorts and board the plane. I am pleased to find the same pilot and staff from yesterday's flight welcoming me. I am told we are destined for Victoria, B.C. and we will be in the air for about seven hours. What is it with me and seven hour flights?

Even though the Agents who drove me here assumed I would be the sole traveller there is one other gentleman already sitting in the passenger section of the plane. Just the two of us to occupy twelve luxurious leather seats. Ah, the life of the rich and famous.

This gentleman nods to me in a friendly way when I pass. I notice he is deeply entrenched in reading what is in front of him. I also note that he is dressed immaculately and I suspect he has an important engagement somewhere on route or in Canada. Government to Government negotiations? A Free Trade conference or dispute? Mutual problems with an ally or, heaven forbid, an enemy? Problems resolving a diplomatic row? There goes me and my imagination again!

This time I am offered breakfast and I manage to eat it without falling asleep and it is delicious. I wash my breakfast down with a second cup of coffee and then engage with a wide variety of reading material that seems to be omnipresent.

About two hours into the flight the other passenger comes over and takes the seat immediately facing me, across a now shared table.

He introduces himself, name missed by me again, and says he is from the White House. He then adds that he is there to debrief me on the events over the last few days and to instruct me on what I can and cannot say about these events. With that introduction he has my full attention. Do I need to change my pants again?

While he goes on in great detail, suffice to say his message is that much of what has transpired over the last several days has to be kept very quiet for political reasons and, apparently, my Government has been apprised and is equally supportive of this prohibition. I am reminded by this gentleman that, even though I am a retired Senior Federal Public Servant, I still carry certain obligations about secrecy and confidentiality. I am reminded I signed an Oath and still hold Secret clearance and hence I am obligated to honour both.

Truth be told, I couldn't give a rat's ass about all this secrecy. I am just happy it is all over and, besides, who would believe me anyway? With that attitude in mind I give the gentleman my assurance. I sign something he puts in front of me. He graciously thanks me and returns to his seat to continue his reading.

The rest of the flight is uneventful. The trip is relaxing and comfortable and I manage to stay awake this time to take in the full experience of travelling in such an extraordinary aircraft. Well, extraordinary to me anyway. Another adventure I will never forget.

The plane arrives in Victoria on schedule and, as I am saying my goodbyes after touch down, the pilot hands me two baseball style ball caps, each adorned with the US Air Force logo, and two sets of replica wings. He says these are with the compliments of the US Airforce. Perfect timing as I didn't have anything for the grandkids. He then smiles rather conspiratorially at me and hands me a bottle of 25-year-old Highland Park. He adds, "Don't tell anybody. We have a pretty good stock on this 'bird' and it won't be missed. From what I can gather you have earned it. Take care, Sir." This is followed by another salute.

I am then politely whisked off the plane and pass quickly through customs. Soon me, my luggage, and all my new swag, are in a taxi heading for my home. With a relaxed sense of personal amusement I contrast this with my last experience in a taxi.

Once we arrive I make sure I get a receipt for the taxi ride. It is an expensive cab trip but I am not put out as I intend to add this to the bill the Senator is racking up.

Finally, unlocking the door to my own house I feel an immense sense of relief. Job done! I can't wait to go pick up Jack and sleep in my own bed.

16

Day Sixteen

I am sitting comfortably in my den, my best buddy Jack at my side, ready to watch a National Address scheduled by the American President or, as I got call him, Charles. I guess referring to him as my friend Chuck would be out of line. Actually, based on what I signed on the plane the other day, I cannot refer to him at all.

This Presidential Address has been rather hurriedly announced and I am more than just a little bit curious as to the subject. Not just because I like to follow US politics but because it follows so closely my recent experiences involving the President and the long held Lincoln secrets. I suspect Lincoln will feature somewhere in the President's remarks.

As the airing begins the President is at his desk in the oval office. A quick camera zoom around the office shows he is accompanied by Wilson Finlayson, his Chief of Staff, by Senator Jefferson Murchison and, somewhat surprisingly, by Emanuel Sayer, Head of the Southern Baptist Coalition.

After a few preliminary remarks, including a well-placed hint that Murchison is about to get his personal endorsement, the President begins his main 'Address:'

> *"My fellow Americans, tonight I want to talk to all of you about gratitude and remorse. Yes, gratitude and remorse. Let me explain!*

"A little over a week ago, Senator Layton Conrad, in a press conference he so guilefully orchestrated, raised a rumour of a questionable nature of which I quote: 'Before he was assassinated, Abraham Lincoln issued some type of formal order stipulating substantial reparations be given to those who were enslaved prior to and during the hostilities of the American Civil War.'

"Senator Conrad went on to add that this rumour also suggested that President Lincoln's promise had enormous financial and land transfer ramifications today.

"Further, the Senator suggested this rumour was a red herring planted by my Party to further divide or confuse the Country. In point of fact he blamed my dear friend here with me tonight, Senator Jefferson Murchison, for starting the rumour. An assigned blame, I would add, for which he has never provided a single shred of evidence.

"Well I am telling you right now, without hesitation, that if this was a red herring, you, Senator Conrad, have the wrong fisherman and the wrong rod. Keeping with this analogy, I tell you now that Senator Conrad was casting in otherwise calm waters trying to get the public to bite on a lure of his own making. Shame on him! Shame on him!

"However, I want to thank him as well. Hold your breath before you think a compliment is coming to Senator Conrad from me. Let me explain.

"Following Senator Conrad's press conference, I was overwhelmed by what I heard, first from History Professor Andrew Hutchins of Stanford University, next from the passionate and heartfelt comments from our dear friend Emanuel Sayer, who is standing here with me this evening, and finally from the thousands of comments, letters and e-mails sent to the White House and reported in the media.

"The White House, and the various media outlets we all listen to, has been inundated with comments about Lincoln's legacy and what may have transpired had he been able to serve his full second term, or maybe even a third or fourth term. The speculation is rife with what would Lincoln have done next? What would he have been able to accomplished?

"The truth is we will never know. But what we do know, what I strongly believe, is that Lincoln cared deeply about the American people both white and black, both northerner and southerner. In his Second

Inauguration Speech, just days before the wars end, he so eloquently spoke on the need to heal, "with malice toward none and with charity for all."

"I firmly believe that had he had the time he would have seized every opportunity to heal, not just the scars caused by four years of war, but by the scars caused by over 200 years of the vileness and obscenity of slavery.

"For those out there who think slavery was a distasteful endeavor practiced by just a few wealthy Southern land owners, think again. Here are a few facts for you to think on.

- *Twelve U.S. presidents owned slaves at some point in their lives; of these, eight owned slaves while in office.*
- *Ten of the first twelve American presidents owned slaves, the only exceptions being John Adams and his son John Quincy Adams, as neither of them approved of slavery.*
- *George Washington was the first president who owned slaves, including while he was president.*
- *Ulysses S. Grant was the last president to have owned slaves at some point in his life.*
- *Of these presidents who owned slaves, Thomas Jefferson owned the most, with more than 500 slaves, followed closely by George Washington.*
- *The 1860 census reported there were 385,000 slave owners in the US and nearly four million slaves. More than one half of all states in the union had some enslaved people in them.*
- *Even Woodrow Wilson was born into a household with slave labor. The Civil War concluded during his childhood but slavery was present in his family's home in his early years.*

"I bet not many of you listening to me tonight were aware of many of those facts I just provided.

"At the end of the Civil War there were suddenly thousands upon thousands of soldiers with uncertain futures, returning to families that may not be there anymore; returning to jobs or farms that may not be there anymore. As tragic and challenging as this was, and it was both tragic and challenging, there were also some four million newly freed slaves who likewise had no land, no work, no farms and seemingly no future.

"I believe that President Lincoln cared deeply about what happened to all those people, again black and white, northerner and southerner.

"Senator Conrad raised the spectre of some type of reparations. We, at the White House, have actually considered this question. Sadly, there

is not enough money in the world that could make up for taking people from their homes and, for decades, forcing them to work in servitude. However, there is also no excuse in the world for the government of the United States of America to not issue an apology, albeit 150 years late, for the treatment that the ancestors of millions of you out there today had to endure

"So today, and I say this with utmost sincerity and humbleness, America is sorry. We are sorry. I am sorry!

"Here in America we are rightly proud of our place in the world, of our democracy, of our leadership and of our influence.

"This country, our Country, the United States of America, is what it is today because of the hard work, care, and dedication of people from all walks of life starting with the original indigenous peoples, then the first colonist arriving on our shores and continuing to all of you listening tonight. But it is also important to recognize that, of those who build this country, millions of those lending a hand or providing the engine of progress were slaves.... and they had no choice.

"While I again reinstate my apology and regret, I also want to express as strongly as I can our 'gratitude.' What an odd concept, gratitude for the enslaved, but gratitude it should be. Perhaps hard to grasp but without the contributions of people who were brought to our shores by force, America would not be what it is today. We need to condemn the heinousness of slavery but we need to acknowledge, with gratitude, the contributions by so many who helped us become who we are today.

"It is worth reminding ourselves that for a great many of the conflicts this great Country has been bravely and steadfastly engaged in since its inception almost 250 years ago many of those engaged in combat were there to fight for our freedom even though 'they had no choice.'

"From the original colonial militias, through the Civil War, through the two Great Wars and into Vietnam many of those fighting for us were conscripted. 'They had no choice.'

"We so gratefully and sincerely celebrate the contributions made by these brave men and women every time we assemble, every time we sing the National Anthem, every November 11, every Memorial Day, and every time we say "thank you for your service." And please remember, as much as we appreciate, value and honour these contributions and these

successes, AND WE SHOULD, understand that for many of those we so honour, they did this even though 'they had no choice.'

"Well, without for one second minimizing the contribution of these millions of brave soldiers over hundreds of years, PLEASE DO NOT THINK I AM, it also has to be said, with gratitude and appreciation, of the contribution of millions of black men, women and children over the several hundred years that we allowed slavery to flourish in America thank you too, even though 'we gave you no choice.'

"What I want you to, need you to, reflect on tonight and, really forever, is that like those we honour who were forced into combat without a choice, those people we enslaved in America also served and contributed.

"To acknowledge America's wilful and vile complicity in the worldwide practice of slavery, but also to acknowledge the contributions made by those enslaved, I have asked Emanuel Sayer of the Southern Baptist Coalition to take the leadership for establishing a National Memorial here in Washington. Perhaps a memorial is not the right term. A visible symbol? I leave that for Emanuel and his team to decide. But, whatever it is to be called, it is to reminds us all of the barbarity of slavery but also of the contributions, albeit forced, those enslaved peoples made to America.

"Millions of you listening tonight have ancestors who faced the obscenity of slavery, and maybe even the sting of the lash, without ever receiving any appreciation or respect for the contributions they made and, indeed, were forced to make, without freedom of choice.

"While it is up to Emanuel and his team to determine 'the what', we will definitely see some type of evocative memorial structure here in D.C. providing a permanent reminder and a compelling acknowledgement of our remorse for the practice of slavery and yet our gratitude for the contributions of those enslaved.

"Anyway, this permanent 'Monument' or 'Symbol' will be there to forever remind us of this sad period of our past but also to recognize the contributions enslaved people made to make this country, our Country, the greatest country on earth.

"Mr. Sayer has already begun to work on this idea and, I believe, he has already got on board a former President and several influential people from the world of business and the world of entertainment to help him with this task. I promise him here tonight, in front of you all, that

I will personally ensure he has all the resources he needs to make this memorial or symbol of remembrance a reality.

"For those of you who may question why tonight, some 150 years after the Emancipation Proclamation, let it be said loudly and clearly, there is no statute of limitations in saying you are sorry! There is no statute of limitations in saying you were wrong! And there is no statute of limitations in saying you are grateful!

"One cannot look forward with complete honesty and commitment until one has looked back and recognized how we got here, both the good and the bad of that earlier journey. This, my friends, is history, and we cannot deny history, no matter how much we may want to or no matter how much some in our Country want to rewrite it to suit their own warped and twisted agendas.

"I would like to conclude by using the words of another great American President, John Fitzgerald Kennedy, who so eloquently said, "As we express our gratitude, we must never forget that the highest appreciation is not to utter words, but to live by them."

"Folks that is my message for the evening, our message for this evening, 'gratitude and remorse.'

"Clearly I have work to do. Emanuel has work to do. So do many, many others. So let us get on with it and move forward in earnest,

"To quote Lincoln once more, let us move forward with 'malice toward none and with charity for all.'

"With that said, I want to wish every one of you good health and prosperity and bid you all a good night."

Having listened intently to every word, I am, at first brush, not sure what to think. In many ways I am very proud of the small contribution my actions over the last while may have contributed, both to the apology and to the idea of a national memorial. However lost in this is any evidence of the Lincoln document itself. I suppose the sound of a paper shredder I thought I heard when leaving the President's office may have been real or, at least, prophetic.

But, when thinking all this over, I also have to conclude that the President did not really have many options in respect to the scale and implications of the reparations the document dictated.

The social and economic disruptions would be so severe that it could further divide, perhaps even permanently divide, an already somewhat troubled nation. Truth be told, I think this President did the right thing by essentially burying the document but still acknowledging many of its intentions.

Being a Canadian, not an American, and certainly not the President, that is all I have to say on the matter. Case closed. The 'buck' doesn't stop with me. It is time to get on with my own life.

Epilogue—several weeks later

A bit of time has passed since the Lincoln document first came to my attention. While I have moved back into a more normal pattern with my life I have not forgotten what happened in the U.K. and in Washington. Those events will always be with me. I have tried to put them behind me as best as I can but they are a part of me now. I will never forget my conversation with the President nor his apology for past American indiscretions.

The President's commitment to the building of a new memorial in D.C. has generally been met with a strong positive public reaction. So too has the President's long overdue apology. His soft pedaling on the subject of reparations, however, has actually been met with an increased call for their consideration. This would seemingly fit in with Senator Murchison's personal point of view. Senator Conrad may rue the day he raised the subject in his press conference. In my highly unqualified opinion, a reparations debate will likely run hot for a while and could even become an election issue. Maybe Lincoln will get his way after all.

Since meeting with Senator Murchison, the Senator has become a conduit and a bit of a friend. He kept his promise to remain in touch. Further, he has kept me informed of what has happened with the co-conspirators.

Gunnar Nielsen and Wyatt Bing have both been charged with murder in the U.K. It seems that the London CCTV cameras clearly picked up both of them entering the bookstore on Charing Cross, putting up the 'closed' sign, and then exiting some twenty minutes later. The CCTV cameras prove that no one else entered the store until the next day when the owner of Heritage Books went in to check on his friend. I am led to believe there was also considerable DNA evidence left behind by those two.

It is expected that both Nielsen and Bing will plead guilty to a lesser charge of Voluntary Manslaughter in exchange for their testimony against Tyrone Thorn. Currently both Nielson and Bing are awaiting extradition to England.

Billy 'Bones' Beaton, Ian Ralston and Ralston's step-brother, Tyrone Thorn, all face various charges associated with assault, kidnapping and conspiracy. Additionally Thorn faces possible murder or manslaughter charges associated with the death of the bookstore owner in the U.K. There is also a potential attempted murder charge associated with the actions he took while holding a weapon to my head in his basement.

Nothing has been able to stick quite firmly enough to the teflon armour surrounding Senator Conrad. No criminal charges are currently being considered. However the media has been sniffing around, a trail of bread crumbs neatly laid out by the White House for them to follow, about his rumoured affiliation with a white supremacist organization called the Brothers of Freedom. Claiming ill health and a desire to move into a new phase of his life he has resigned his seat in the Senate and states emphatically that he has no intention of ever running for public office again. There is a further trail of evidence just waiting to unfold should he ever fail to keep his promise.

Senator Murchison skillfully skirted the issue of his hiring of Ian Ralston as his Director of Communications by asserting, quite publicly, that he knew all along that Ralston was connected with the Brothers of Freedom. He avows he fed Ralston false leads so that he could catch him out and thereby expose him and the Brotherhood. Of course, he is loudly applauding his own success in this regard and, in his words, states "I caught the bastard red-handed." His popularity seems to have gone up a notch as a result.

The origin of all these charges, the Lincoln Document itself, strangely was never made mention of in all the fallout. It seems just like it never existed. The charges all seem to revolve around allegations of the stealing of mysterious 'government secrets.'

On the home front, after a few less than successful attempts at the outset, I have been able to establish regular contact with Darcy. She is, in fact, flying over next Tuesday to spend a week here with me. Things look much rosier. I told her that the bruises on my chest, where she hit me after she got out of the trunk of her car, have almost healed. She didn't think that was funny but has promised to kiss it better if I behave myself. Is it time to speed up the 'take-it-slow' agenda? I sure hope so.

The kids and grandkids are all fine. Jack is still announcing his presence with authority at every opportunity. And I have a nice new wardrobe consisting of Ferragamo loafers, a Brooks Brother jacket and a Burberry tie, capped off with a White House tie pin.

I think I will wear this ensemble the first night Darcy arrives when I take her out for dinner. Actually maybe on the second night as I have, fingers crossed, firmer plans for the first night... nudge, nudge, wink, wink.

Finally, to put an end to this saga, I have to confess that securely stowed away in my small home safe is a three page document I received from the expert in Alnwick, Thomas Rhodes. This previously undisclosed document is a written record of the authentication process Thomas Rhodes conducted. It guarantees the authentication of the Lincoln Executive Order aka 'the Lincoln Promise.' It is signed by all four people who were consulted and confirms their concurrence in the authentication process. Further, Thomas Rhodes had it duly notarized by a lawyer the evening before I picked it up in Alnwick.

More importantly, resting in this small safe of mine, just below these three pages from Thomas Rhodes, is the original and authentic Lincoln document itself. If you recall, I had three copies made. The first copy I sent by overnight courier to Senator Murchison. The second copy I gave to Bevis and Butthead in trade to rescue Darcy. The third, I assume, is in shreds at the bottom of the waste bin in the President's den at the White House or met a similar fate elsewhere.

It seems nobody ever looks inside anybody else's golf bag. That is where I stowed these two valuable documents. My clubs arrived safely at my house a week after I got home from D.C. The cost of the third mortgage on my house to pay for the shipping of my golf clubs was worth every penny. Now if I could just figure out what happened to my 9-iron?

You see, believing so passionately in my sister Maureen's dedication to our family's ancestry, I have come to understand that you have to respect, protect and retain what the family bequeaths to you no matter what it may be and, after all, Abe is family. Don't worry cousin Abe, I have you covered!

Now it seems like a good time to take Jack for a walk. Here, boy! Let's go!

Author's note

The Lincoln Promise is a work of pure fiction. Any resemblance of the characters in this book to any living person or persons is strictly coincidental, with the exception that people who do know me well may find some similarities between some of the family of the protagonist, Jay Alexander, and my own family. These familial similarities are used to provide a believable background for the protagonist and to acknowledge my wonderful family. To illustrate, I did have a sister named Maureen. She did have a keen interest in Genealogy. She has, very sadly, passed away. And, to anyone who knew her, she was an amazing person and a true force of nature.

As for other genealogical references, those regarding Lincoln are entirely fictitious. We are not related. However the author does have a confirmed familial connection with the poet Robbie Burns and there is some yet-to-be confirmed conjecture that the author's family may have connections to both Warkworth and Alnwick castles.

While the quote regarding the Emancipation Proclamation and Lincoln's response to Horace Greeley (chapter 1) are factual, and presented accurately, the document referred to as the 49th Executive Order is entirely made up by the author. There is no evidence that this Executive Order, or anything resembling it, exits now or ever. Other data respecting the 1860 census, and the ownership of slaves by former Presidents, are based on a variety of sources that I believe to be accurate.

As for some of the geographical locations mentioned in the book, Alnmouth and Alnwick are indeed real places and are, in my opinion, wonderful places to visit should the opportunity arise. I have taken some small liberties in describing certain elements of the village of Alnmouth and the market town of Alnwick. These are minor and only to enhance the story.

There is indeed an excellent book store in Alnwick, Barter Books. It is worth a visit, including a stop at their café. The book store is located in an elegant old train station. I have no idea whether or not they can authenticate very old documents but they do have many rare and vintage books for sale.

The London streets and tube stations named in this book are real. The tourist sites named in both London and York are also very real and are also very much worth a visit or two, in my opinion.

Throughout this book several references are made to famous movies, popular music and famous duos, comedic or cartoon. These references are made to include pop culture in the conversations and thoughts of the protagonist and other characters in the book just as these types of reference might be made in any day-to-day conversations between people. Pop culture is just that, pop culture, and is part of our day-to-day communication.

Acknowledgments

Thanks must go to Dorothy for her patience, support and editorial assistance as I was writing this book. Thanks also go to our friend, Tony Burton, for his editorial support and his guiding me as I embarked on my first experience with the publication process.

Author

James (Jim) Brown was born and raised in New Westminster, B.C. and has lived his whole live in B.C. Although he has written for fun for years, this is Jim's first published novel. Currently he and his wife, Dorothy, reside on a small acreage on Vancouver Island, along with two cats, a variable number of horses, and a dog named Winston. Surprisingly perhaps, Winston is not a Jack Russell Terrier. Dorothy and Jim have two children, a son and a daughter, as well as three grandchildren.

Jim is one of five siblings. As in the book, he did indeed have three older sisters as well as one younger brother. Sadly two of his older sisters, Maureen and Doreen, have passed away. This book is dedicated to their memories. The courage and determination shown by the protagonist in this book is reflective of these same characteristics shown through the lives of these two special women. They both lived their lives with love, kindness, compassion and courage. Perhaps the quote from Lincoln featured in the book describes them well, 'With malice toward none and with charity to all.'

Made in United States
Troutdale, OR
06/04/2024

20317124R10116